"Zach Collingsworth," he said. "I'm a neighbour, and I'd feel a bit more welcome if you'd aim that gun in another direction."

"You're Zach?" she said, sounding a bit shocked. Guess he'd changed in fifteen years, as well. Unfortunately, the gun was still aimed right between his eyes.

"I heard you had some trouble last night. I came over to see if I can help."

"That's nice of you, but everything's under control."

"Not if you plan on shooting everyone who stops by."

"Not everyone," she said, "just the ones who look like trouble."

But his new voluptuous neighbour had finally lowered the gun. He took that for an invitation, so he grinned and headed for her porch. Suddenly renewing old friendships and offering comfort didn't seem such a bad idea after all.

CAST OF CHARACTERS

Kali Cooper – She's just inherited the Silver Spurs Ranch and trying desperately to keep it.

Zach Collingsworth – The youngest of the four Collingsworth brothers.

Langston, Matt and Bart Collingsworth – Zach's three brothers.

Lenora Collingsworth – Zach's mother and acting CEO of Collingsworth Enterprises.

Jeremiah Collingsworth – Zach's grandfather who is recovering from a stroke.

Randolph Collingsworth – Lenora's beloved husband who has been dead for over twenty years.

Aidan Jefferies – Houston homicide detective and good friend to Langston Collingsworth.

Billy Mack – Neighbouring rancher.

Ed Guerra – Local sheriff.

Gordon Cooper – Kali's late grandfather and previous owner of the Silver Spurs Ranch.

Tony Pinter – Foreman of Silver Spurs Ranch when Gordon Cooper was alive.

Gerald Pinter – Tony Pinter's son.

Hade Carpenter – Gordon Cooper's stepson, and second in line to inherit the Silver Spurs Ranch.

Point Blank Protector

JOANNA WAYNE

MILLS & BOON
Pure reading pleasure™

*First published in Great Britain 2009
by Harlequin Mills & Boon Limited,
Eton House, 18-24 Paradise Road, Richmond, Surrey TW9 1SR*

© Jo Ann Vest 2008

ISBN: 978 0 263 87300 9

46-0609

*Printed and bound in Spain
by Litografia Rosés S.A., Barcelona*

ABOUT THE AUTHOR

Joanna Wayne was born and raised in Shreveport, Louisiana, and received her undergraduate and graduate degrees from LSU-Shreveport. She moved to New Orleans in 1984, and it was there that she attended her first writing class and joined her first professional writing organisation. Her first novel, *Deep in the Bayou*, was published in 1994.

Now, dozens of published books later, Joanna has made a name for herself as being on the cutting edge of romantic suspense in both series and single-title novels. She has been on the Waldenbooks bestsellers list for romance and has won many industry awards. She is a popular speaker at writing organisations and local community functions and has taught creative writing at the University of New Orleans Metropolitan College.

She currently resides in a small community forty miles north of Houston, Texas, with her husband. Though she still has family and emotional ties to Louisiana, she loves living in the Lone Star state. You may write to Joanna at PO Box 265, Montgomery, Texas 77356, USA.

This book is for all my Texas friends who have taught me about the ranching lifestyle and to every woman who enjoys reading about cowboy heroes. And a kiss to my hubby for not complaining when I became so engrossed in writing the book that I forgot to cook dinner.

Prologue

The night was pitch-black when Kali Cooper stepped out of her mud-encrusted Jeep to open the gate to the Silver Spurs Ranch. *Her* ranch.

She still hadn't quite gotten her mind around the fact that she was the actual owner of the spread she'd loved since her first and only visit fifteen years ago. But after months of court battles with the son of her late grandfather's third wife, it was official.

Grandfather Gordy's will had been clear and absolutely legal. As long as she lived on the land for a year, it was hers. She planned to live here forever.

The wind cut through her denim jacket and she could smell the approaching rain. She picked up her pace as lightning cut a jagged scar across the night sky followed by a loud clap of thunder.

The weather channel had predicted a line of moderate to severe storms followed by an arctic cold front that was dipping all the way to the Gulf of Mexico and bringing with it temperatures near the freezing mark. Even for mid-February, that was cold for the Houston area.

Wings fluttered above her and something rustled the grass as the gate swung open and clanked against the metal post. An eerie uneasiness crept along her nerve endings along with the awareness of just how alone she really was. According to her research, the closest ranch was Jack's Bluff, owned by the very wealthy Collingsworth family, and even as the crow flies, that was over a mile away.

She hurried back to the Jeep, drove across the cattle gap then jumped out to close and latch the heavy metal gate. Five minutes later, she pulled up in front of the old homestead.

Caught in the ghostly glow of her headlights, the one-story structure seemed to crawl out at odd angles from the front porch. It was smaller than she remembered it, but then thanks to the feud between her father and grandfather, she hadn't been here since she was eleven.

That was the summer she'd experienced her first case of serious puppy love. The object of her affections had been Zach Collingsworth, and she'd fawned and drooled over him like the naive kid she'd been. Here's hoping he wouldn't remember her. With luck, he'd also be paunchy and balding, with a wife and several kids.

She reached for her flashlight and was about to kill the engine and cut off the lights when she saw what appeared to be a person running from the house.

Panic shot through her, but when another streak of lightning made the scene as bright as day, all she saw were tree branches swaying in the wind.

She really was letting the isolation get to her. The house was empty and had been for months. The livestock had been sold and the help let go when her grandfather had died.

She stepped from the car just as lightning struck again, this time a dazzling needle of electricity that followed a direct path from sky to ground and seemed to strike mere yards away. The thunder that followed was deafening.

The first drops of rain pricked Kali's face as she made a wild dash for the covered porch. She was stamping the mud from her boots when her gaze caught and held. She stared, at first not willing to believe her eyes, but the stream of crimson spilling out the door was all too vivid.

Her heart slammed against her chest, and this time she didn't try to convince herself she was imagining things. She started to run and was almost to her car before her powers of reason pushed through the adrenaline rush.

Paint—not blood. That was it, of course. She sucked in a huge gulp of damp air as the picture became crystal-clear. Hade Carpenter only lost the ranch to her if she lived here for a full year. He probably planned to make sure she didn't last a night, so he'd come out here with his Halloweenish tricks to frighten her away. Nice try, but it wouldn't work.

Bracing herself for what she'd find inside, she marched back to the porch and turned the doorknob. The door was unlocked and it creaked and whined open at her touch.

One look inside and she knew the blood was real.

Chapter One

Lenora Collingsworth loved frigid Saturday mornings when her family gathered around the huge stone fireplace in the family den instead of all going their separate ways. Not that she didn't love spring and fall. Even hot south Texas summers had their high points, but still there was something special about having all your children warmed by the same crackling blaze.

Her twin grandsons were missing for the moment, having donned their jackets and escaped out the back door to toss around a football and have a good excuse to tackle and scuffle. David and Derrick were seven years old and a joy to have around.

Still it broke Lenora's heart that her oldest daughter was separated from their father. The boys needed him. So did Becky for that matter. The problem was she'd married a man as stubborn as she was.

So Becky and the boys were back on Jack's Bluff Ranch with the rest of the Collingsworth clan. Well, technically, Langston didn't live at the ranch. He and his wife Trish and their teenage daughter Gina lived in Houston during the week. His duties as president of Collingsworth Oil pretty much demanded it, but they spent most weekends at the ranch.

And much to Lenora's delight, Trish was pregnant. She couldn't wait to cuddle a grandchild in her arms again. She'd already pulled the antique cradle that all her children had slept in from storage. Their neighbor Billy Mack was restoring it.

She was lucky her children were tied to the land and family but still independent with minds of their own and clear goals for their lives. At least most of them were. At twenty-six, Zach and Jaime didn't seem tied to anything but having a good time.

Jaime was a free spirit. Zach was her jet-setter. Except for a couple of brief stints working for Collingsworth Oil, Zach had spent the two years since graduating from the University of Texas roaming Europe. Getting the feel for the foreign business relations he'd majored in, he claimed.

As far as she could tell, most of the relations he'd explored had been with beautiful young females and the business had been that of enjoying himself immensely. But even with the extensive travels, he'd retained his cowboy charm. Jack's Bluff definitely got into a person's blood.

Nonetheless, the bottom line was that it was past time for Jaime and Zach to get their acts together.

She'd love to see them settle in the way Bart and

Matt had. Both worked full time running the ranch and had built homes right here at Jack's Bluff. Bart lived with his new wife Jaclyn on Scuttle Creek. Jaclyn was a dear and the perfect mate for Bart.

Matt lived alone in a rambling structure built on the edge of the woods and overlooking a waterhole favored by the many deer in the area. She had high hopes he'd find his soul mate soon, but for now he seemed perfectly happy without one.

Lenora went to the kitchen for a refill on hot chocolate and brought the pot back to the den with her. "More cocoa, anyone?"

"Thanks, Grandma. I'd love more," Gina said, lifting her blue pottery mug and then groaning as Jaime placed the letters Z, A and X on the Scrabble board.

"You better watch Jaime," Zach said. "I hate to say it but I'm certain my twin sister cheats. That's the only way she could ever have beaten me at anything."

"It's called division of the genes," Jaime scoffed. "You got the brawn. I got the brains—and the good looks."

"In your dreams."

The doorbell rang. They all looked up, though no one made a move toward the door.

"Is anyone expecting company?" Lenora asked.

No one was. Langston folded the section of the *Houston Chronicle* he'd been reading, stood and started to the door. "It's probably just Billy Mack."

Lenora thought he was likely right. Their neighbor had taken to coming around a lot more often of late.

Living alone had to be tough on him. Not that he'd ever admit it.

But the booming voice she heard next didn't belong to Billy Mack. A few seconds later Langston ushered Sheriff Ed Guerra into the den.

"I hate to bust in on you like this," Ed said, "but there's a problem over at the Silver Spurs Ranch. I thought you should be alerted."

"What kind of problem?" Langston asked.

"Guess you know that Gordon Cooper's granddaughter inherited his spread."

"We heard that months ago," Lenora said, "but apparently there were some kinks in the will that had to be ironed out."

"She got here last night," the sheriff said, "and her welcome to Colts Run Cross wasn't the most hospitable."

Bart stepped over to where Langston and the sheriff were standing. "How inhospitable are we talking?"

"As in there was a body with a couple of bullet holes in it waiting for her just inside the door."

Lenora's chest tightened, and her gaze went immediately to Gina. She wasn't sure her teenage granddaughter needed to hear Ed's uncensored version of this. Trish had obviously decided the same thing. She was already doing the boot-scoot routine with Gina to get her through the doorway that led to the kitchen.

"Gina and I will make coffee," Trish said.

Ed gave her an understanding nod. "Best idea I

heard today." He waited until she and Gina were out of sight. "The rest of you females might want to join them. This ain't a pretty story."

"Can't be worse than the nightly news," Jaime said. "Besides, if there's a murderer in our midst, we're going to hear about it soon enough."

"You can be sure of that. But you folks being the closest neighbors, I thought I should tell you about it first. Thought maybe you could check in on Kali Cooper, too. She's pretty shaken up by this—not that I blame her none. Poor lady's single and staying out there by herself."

"Why don't you take a seat and start at the beginning?" Matt said.

Ed dropped to the corner of the couch, took off his worn black Western hat and held it in his lap, fingering the brim as he talked. "I got a call from the 911 operator about midnight, right in the thick of the storm. She said she had a frantic caller on the phone claiming she was standing over a murder victim."

Lenora was sucked into the dread as she listened to the rest of the story. How frightening for a young woman to walk into what she thought was an empty house and find that macabre scene waiting for her. "How old is Kali Cooper?"

"Twenty-six," Ed said. "The victim looks to be even younger. She might even be a teenager."

Maybe as young as her granddaughter Gina. A bone-chilling shiver climbed Lenora's spine. "Do you know the identity of the victim?"

"Not yet, but we do know that no one's been reported missing from our immediate area."

"How long had she been dead?" Matt asked.

"Best estimate is that she was shot within an hour of the time Kali arrived on the scene. Kali was damned lucky she didn't walk in on the killing. If she had we'd likely be investigating two murders today."

Becky walked to the window and looked out. Lenora knew she was assuring herself the boys were fine.

"Kali must be horrified." Jaime said.

"Yeah, but that girl's got grit. She stayed at the motel in town last night. I didn't want her living in the crime scene until we had a chance to comb it thoroughly. But I gave her clearance to return an hour ago, and she's already back on the premises."

"Zach can go check on her," Lenora said.

"I knew I could count on you folks for that," Ed said. "And until we get a handle on things, it wouldn't hurt to be careful, especially you women. No tellin' where the killer is now."

Lenora stayed back as her three oldest sons walked to the front door with the sheriff, Matt still asking questions.

Zach propped a booted foot on the hearth. "How did I get elected to go check on the new neighbor?"

"You and Kali are the same age and you played together when you were children."

"That was fifteen years ago."

"See, you remember her, and I'm sure she'll remember you. Having a friend show up after last night will be more reassuring than having a stranger show up at her door."

"I remember her because she was as annoying as a burr in a sock and kept following me around."

"You're exaggerating."

"He's shaking in his boots," Jaime teased. "Want me to tag along and protect you?"

"Scared has nothing to do with it. I just don't like calming hysterical women. What if she starts crying?"

"Hand her a tissue," Lenora said. "And don't come on to her. This isn't the time for that."

"Give me a little credit." Zach left through the kitchen door, but returned a second later wearing a black leather jacket and holding his Stetson.

"That was quick," Jaime said. "I think your complaints were camouflage. Looks to me like you're eager to hook up with this old flame."

"I'm just going to get my neighborly duties over with before Mom hands me a basket of goodies to deliver."

"Great idea," Lenora said. "Juanita baked yesterday and there should be plenty of the lemon tea cakes left."

Zach groaned. "This isn't a tea party."

"You win, Zach. I'll give her the cookies later, but I want you to insist she join us for dinner tonight. If she's afraid to stay on the ranch alone, just bring her back with you now."

"Okay, but if she's as weird as she was as a kid and starts stalking me, it's on your conscience."

"I'll live with it," Lenora said, smiling. "But be careful, Zach, and I don't mean of Kali."

"If you're worried, you can send Matt. He's older and—well, he's older."

"You'll do fine. Just be careful."

But he was already heading for the back door, his cocky swagger a discomforting reminder that he wasn't afraid of anything and that being wary would never cross his mind. Maybe sending him to see Kali wasn't the best idea after all.

"Relax, Mom," Jaime said, no doubt reading her concern. "I'm sure the killer is long gone. If he wasn't, Sheriff Guerra would already have him in custody."

"That makes sense," Lenora said. Still she worried. It was her job. She was a mother.

ZACH WAS not looking forward to playing comforter to Kali Cooper, but he'd love to go toe to toe with the cowardly skunk who'd murdered a young woman. He hadn't wanted to belabor the point with his mother or Jaime, but what kind of deranged pervert got his rocks off like that?

Zach kept his eyes peeled for anything suspicious as he made the short drive to the Silver Spurs Ranch. He'd taken Bart's pickup truck instead of his own new Jaguar. The main roads at Jack's Bluff were graded regularly and kept in excellent condition, but the ones at the Silver Spurs were another story.

He slowed as he turned right on Cooper's Road. That wasn't the official name of the blacktop that dead ended at the front entrance to the Silver Spurs Ranch, but that was the only thing Zach or probably anyone else around here had ever heard it called. And there was no road sign to suggest they were wrong.

The fence posts along the edge of the road were leaning and there were several breaks in the strings of barbed wire. Old man Cooper had kept the place in top-notch shape when he was able, but it had fallen into disrepair when his health had started to fail, and it had gone downhill even faster during the months since his death.

That might explain why a killer had found his way to the spot. He could have gotten lost and wound up on the dead-end road. One look and he'd have figured that the ranch was deserted.

The gate was open and banging in the wind when Zach reached it. He drove through, then got out of his truck and closed and latched it. Not that there were any livestock to worry about or that closing it would deter a killer, but latching gates was a habit everyone growing up on a ranch learned early in life.

As he'd suspected, the ranch road was a muddy slush and he dodged potholes and trenches where the squad cars had slewed around them. He wondered as he did what a city girl was going to do in a place like this. He could imagine her now, traipsing through the mud in fancy, high-heeled boots with her skinny arms swinging at her side and her red hair flying about like a horse's mane.

Probably more of a pain now than she'd been that

long-ago summer when she'd followed him around like a sick calf. Still, he felt bad that she'd arrived to a bloody welcome.

He pulled up in front of the house and was about to step out of the pickup when the front door of the house flew open. A young woman stepped onto the porch with a shotgun in hand. If the woman was Kali, she looked a lot different all grown up.

He climbed from behind the wheel and waved a greeting. "Zach Collingsworth," he said. "I'm a neighbor, and I'd feel a bit more welcome if you'd aim that gun in another direction."

"You're Zach?" she said, sounding a bit shocked. Guess he'd changed in fifteen years as well. Unfortunately, the gun was still aimed at his eyeballs.

"I heard you had some trouble last night. I came over to see if I can help."

"That's nice of you, but everything's under control."

"Not if you plan on shooting everyone who stops by."

"Not everyone," she said, "just the ones who look like trouble."

But his new voluptuous neighbor had finally lowered the gun. He took that for an invitation, so he grinned and headed for her porch. Suddenly renewing old friendships and offering comfort didn't seem like such a bad idea after all.

Chapter Two

"I really am okay," Kali said, when Zach joined her on the porch.

"I believe you, but since I'm here you might as well invite me in."

"The house isn't exactly ready for guests."

"That's okay, as long as you don't expect me to grab a mop."

"I make no promises, but if you're not afraid of dirt and bugs, come on in."

The front door opened directly into a large dark-paneled room with a brick fireplace. The heavy oak tables, two brown tweed sofas and a couple of rocking chairs were covered in a thick layer of Texas dust and a substance Zach guessed to be fingerprint powder.

The windows were so streaked with grime that the bright rays of late-morning sunshine could barely fight their way through. Worse, every nook and cranny sported a filigreed network of spiderwebs.

"I see what you mean," he said. "No offense but

the place looks like a haunted house at an amusement park."

Only this time the dead body had been real. And Kali had walked in on the scene late at night and in the middle of a thunderstorm. He'd have expected her to be speeding down the Interstate by now heading back to wherever it was she'd come from. Instead she was swatting at a wasp that had just dive-bombed her.

Zach picked up one of the stained towels she'd obviously been using for cleaning and slammed it and the wasp against the wall. When the struggling insect fell to the floor, he squashed it under the toe of his boot. "Save you from having to waste a shotgun shell on him," he teased.

"Not funny."

She was right, he decided as he eyed the bloodstain on the floor. "Your arrival last night must have been a shocker."

"To say the least."

"Yet you came back out here today. That takes guts."

"I don't have a choice. I quit my job in Atlanta and sold everything I owned except my Jeep and the belongings I could stuff into it so that I'd have funds to get the Silver Spurs up and running again."

"Surely you're not planning to do that by yourself?"

Her eyebrows arched. "You think I can't because I'm a woman?"

A loaded question that called for an evasive answer. "I just wondered if... I wondered if you were married." A blatant lie, but better than getting her riled.

"I'm not married, but I'm not some helpless Southern belle, either. I'm used to taking care of myself."

In town, maybe, but out here? He had his doubts. "Ranching is a competitive business these days. If you're set on trying it, I'd suggest you hire someone who knows cattle. My brothers Bart and Matt might have some recommendations for a foreman. You should check with them."

"I'll keep that in mind, but my first priority will be making the house livable. I was pleasantly surprised when the sheriff gave me permission to return to the ranch today."

"Ed Guerra might talk like an unsophisticated cowboy sheriff, but he knows his stuff."

"I guess. It's just that…"

Her words ran out and vulnerability seeped into the depths of her caramel-colored eyes. Zach shifted his weight to the other foot and hoped she didn't go all emotional on him.

"The body was right there," Kali said, pointing to the bloodstain near the front door. "It was as if the killer had just dragged her inside to shoot her."

Or that she was trying to escape and he stopped her. "Did you hear shots?"

"If I had, I would have thought it was thunder. The storm had turned violent at that point."

"Were there any signs that the killer and victim might have been camping out in the house?"

"The sheriff asked that same question, but I really

don't think anyone had been staying here. There was no food in the cabinets and no sheets on the beds. And the electricity had been off until I had it turned on last week."

"What about the water from the faucet? Was it clear or did it have that rusty look from sitting in the pipes too long?"

"I'm not sure. The sheriff rushed me out before I had a chance to try it." She took a deep breath and exhaled slowly. "I'm sorry, Zach, but I really don't want to talk about the murder anymore today. I've already gone over every detail with the sheriff."

Reluctantly, Zach changed the subject. He walked to the window and looked out at the high grass and the overgrown weeds. "You could use a bush hog."

"I'm not planning to raise any kind of hogs."

"You don't raise a bush hog. It's a rotary cutter that can take care of the low brush, weeds and grass in no time. I'm sure your grandfather had one. It's likely in the metal storage building, but you'll need someone to operate it for you."

"I'll check it out once I get the house and stables in order. I'm hoping to bring in the first horses by the end of the month and be open for business by the first of April."

"Business?"

"Right. The Silver Spurs Riding Stables and Horseman Training Center. It has a nice ring to it, don't you think?"

"Is that because your grandfather raised a few horses?"

"No, it's because it's what I choose to do."

She turned her back on him, picked up a broom that had been leaning against the hearth and started knocking spiderwebs from the ceiling. Her hair fell down her back, the multiple layers of auburn locks swishing back and forth with the motion of her body. Even her hair was different from the wild red tangles he remembered. It was a gorgeous auburn color now and smelled of spring flowers.

None of which meant she knew a thing about horses. "What qualifies you to teach horsemanship?"

"I've taught at a private stable just outside Atlanta for the past four years." Her tone registered her irritation with his question.

"Teaching at some fancy city stable is a lot different than running a ranch operation."

She set the broom back on the floor, but held on to it. "I appreciate your coming by to check on me, Zach, but I really don't have time for your negativism and I do have to get back to work. Let yourself out, will you?"

Before he could reply, she walked away and left him standing in the middle of the den floor. He had a feeling her irritation had as much to do with the situation as with him, though he could have been a bit more tactful.

He started to leave, then remembered the rest of the reason he'd been sent to visit Kali. He wandered to the back of the house and found her in the kitchen pouring liquid detergent into a large bucket.

"Mom asked me to invite you to dinner tonight," he said.

She dipped a rag into the soap mixture, then wrung it dry. "Tell your mother I appreciate the invitation, but that I didn't get a lot of sleep last night. I plan to go to bed early tonight."

"I'll tell her, but she doesn't give up that easily. If you don't go to dinner, she'll likely bring dinner to you."

Kali straightened and turned to face him, her enticing breasts pushing against the fabric of her hot-pink T-shirt. "Was it your mother's idea for you to come over and check on me, Zach?"

"Actually it was the sheriff's idea. He thought you might still be upset over finding the body last night."

"Of course I'm upset. Any sane person would be, but I'm not going to fall apart if that's what you think."

"I don't, but…"

"But what?"

But now that he was thinking about it again, it didn't seem safe for her to stay here alone. "You might sleep better if you stay at our place tonight. There's plenty of room."

"Was that the sheriff's idea, too?"

"No, that one was all mine."

"Thanks," she said, sounding as if she meant it. "But the sheriff says he's going to have a deputy keep an eye on my place tonight. And I have the shotgun. Besides, I have to stay alone sooner or later. If you fall off a horse, you get right back on."

"We're not talking horses."

"It's the same principle. I'll be okay, Zach. Tell your mother I'll take her up on the dinner invitation soon. And she doesn't need to worry about me starving tonight. I stopped at Thompson's Grocery this morning and stocked up on food."

"Sounds as if you're all set." He smiled, tipped his hat and took the back door out of the house. No use to chance putting his foot in his mouth again and wearing out his welcome on his first visit.

His thoughts zeroed in on the murder as he left. He couldn't see a man driving all the way from Houston to the Silver Spurs in a storm just to shoot a woman.

And what rotten timing for Kali. She'd moved to one of the most crime-free idyllic areas in the state only to step right into the path of a killer.

He was glad his mother had insisted he check on her. Kali wasn't the svelte, sophisticated model-type beauty he usually dated, but she had that healthy girl-next-door-thing going on.

He might consider coming over here and actually doing a little physical labor himself except that he'd just taken a position at Collingsworth Oil that required his presence at the Houston office Monday through Friday. Not that she'd miss him. There would be plenty of eager cowboys to take his place.

He still thought his offer of her spending the night at Jack's Bluff made sense, but admittedly there was no real reason to think the killer would return unless…

Unless the killer actually *was* a deranged pervert and knew Kali was living alone on the isolated ranch. That thought continued to haunt him as he drove the few miles back to Jack's Bluff.

WORK MADE the day pass all too quickly and it was dusk before Kali took her first break. She poured herself a cup of tea and collapsed onto the wooden rocker that she'd polished to a glossy shine.

The room looked a hundred percent better than it had this morning. The sofas' worn upholstery was shampooed, and the ragged, dust-infused cotton throw rugs were resting in the bottom of the trash. A bedroom and the house's one bathroom were just as clean. She'd tackle the kitchen tomorrow.

The floorboards creaked beneath the movement of the rocker. She shifted and her gaze fell on the spot where she'd scrubbed the blood from the floorboards. The stain had almost completely disappeared, yet the scene she'd walked in on materialized vividly in her mind, sending a foreboding chill through her bloodstream.

Kali took a deep breath that did little to settle her nerves, then grabbed her jacket and walked onto the porch for a bracing breath of cold air. She'd managed to keep the disturbing thoughts and fearsome questions at bay while she was struggling with the

cleaning chores. Now they were claiming her mind
and tightening her sore, aching muscles.

She closed the door behind her and leaned against
the porch railing, staring at the dirt drive that led
away from the house and meandered its lonely way
to the highway. The isolation closed in on her, attack-
ing her self confidence. Perhaps she'd been too hasty
in turning down Zach's offer to spend the night with
his family at Jack's Bluff.

Zach Collingsworth. His name played in her mind,
then slipped from her lips with the frosty vapors of
her breath. She'd wondered what it would be like to
see him again, had thought she might not even recognize him. Mainly she'd hoped that the childish
crush would seem stupid and something to laugh
about now that they were both in their mid twenties.

She should have been so lucky.

At eleven he'd been cute. Now he was—in a
word—gorgeous. Thick, dark hair, cut stylishly
short, but long enough that a woman could sink her
fingers into it. Lean, not too tall, but tall enough. He
looked like a model, yet with that cowboy edge that
made him reek of sensuality.

And here she went, falling into the same Zach
trap that she had years ago. But she couldn't give in
to the mind-numbing attraction this time. She needed
all her wits about her. She had one year to make a go
of the riding stables and training center before she ran
out of money. One short year to make her dream a
reality—or see it die.

Pulling her jacket around her, she gave a last look into the growing darkness, then turned and went back inside. The piercing jangle of her cell phone startled her and sent her rushing to the kitchen to find it amidst the cleaning supplies.

"Hello."

"Howdy."

Kali recognized the deep, slightly crusty voice even before the sheriff finished identifying himself.

"How are things going out at the Silver Spurs?"

"Fine, so far."

"That's good to hear."

"Do you have any leads on a suspect?" she asked, hoping that was why he'd called.

"No, but I thought you might like to know that we've identified the body. The woman's name is Louisa Kellogg."

"Is she from Colts Run Cross?"

"No. She was a student at the University of Houston. That's about all I know for now, but I'm hoping we have some of the killer's DNA on her somewhere. If not, there's a good chance we have fingerprints from your door or the light switch, maybe even from the walls."

"Have you questioned anyone about her?"

"Not yet, but don't you worry. We'll catch the killer. Right now I just want to make sure you're doing okay."

Apprehension shook her resolve. "Why? Have you changed your mind about it being safe for me to stay here?"

"Not at all. The killer's likely from Houston just like his victim. He'll probably stay way the hell away from the scene of the crime—pardon my French. In case he doesn't, one of my best-trained deputies is keeping an eye on your place tonight."

"I appreciate that."

"Just don't shoot him if he shines a light around the house to check things out. He ain't much to look at, but his wife still likes having him around."

She smiled at the sheriff's humor in spite of the fear that pummeled her nerves. Once she'd said goodbye and broken the connection, she struggled to push the situation to the back corners of her mind.

She should fix something to eat and have a glass of wine, but first she needed a bath. The layers of dust and grime she'd cleaned from the house seemed embedded in her skin.

She walked to the bathroom, turned on the faucet and stripped off her jeans, T-shirt and undies. Exhausted, she stepped into the claw-footed tub and sank into the hot water. By the time she'd lathered every inch of her body, she was so weary she could barely think.

She'd forgotten to unpack the towels she'd brought with her so she padded to the bedroom for her old yellow fleece robe, dripping as she went. She snuggled into the robe and fell across the bed.

The wind picked up, rattling the windows and pushing cold drafts around the sills. She closed her eyes, half expecting images of Louisa Kellogg's body to creep into her mind.

Instead it was Zach Collingsworth's face that pushed through the fog of fatigue. As far as her heart was concerned, he might be the most dangerous dream of all.

THE COLLINGSWORTH Sunday brunch had its roots more in a bribe than a treat for the taste buds. Lenora's faith was all-important to her and when she'd first married Randolph she'd wanted him to share it. She'd promised to cook anything and everything he wanted if he'd go to church with her.

Reluctantly, he'd agreed, but he'd put her to the test week after week, requesting one gourmet entree after another. The bribe had been a success on several levels. Randolph had eventually embraced her faith in God, her cooking skills had improved dramatically and the Collingsworth family brunch had become entrenched in their routine.

A few years back, Lenora's children had persuaded her to hire a cook so that she could have more time for herself. Now Sunday was the only day Lenora took over her kitchen. She made the most of it by planning ahead and delegating duties so that in under an hour after returning from early services at their church, the family was gathered at the table. She always served up old favorites and a couple of surprises. Today the surprises were crab bisque and raspberry scones topped with Chantilly cream.

The doorbell rang just as her father-in-law Jeremiah finished saying grace, his voice growing so steady of late that at times he sounded almost like the pre-stroke Jeremiah.

"That's probably Melvin," Langston said. "He was supposed to get back from a business trip to Dubai last night, and he said he was hungry for Texas cooking."

Lenora started to go for another plate, but her daughter Becky beat her to the task. Billy Mack, a brunch regular, scooted over a bit and made room for the extra chair Bart was already sliding into place.

Melvin was Langston's right-hand man at Collingsworth Oil. Jeremiah had hired him without consulting Langston, but Melvin had immediately proved his worth by suggesting changes that had increased their profits on a drilling project in the Gulf of Mexico by twenty percent.

But that was business. It was his ready smile and terrific sense of humor that had let him work his way into the family circle.

Jeremiah reached for the plate of scrambled eggs that was just out of his reach. "You guys gonna pass food or just play musical chairs?"

"Yeah," Derrick said. "I'm starved."

"You are always starved," Bart said, teasing his young nephew. "You can tell you're kin to your uncle Matt."

"Ranchers need stamina," Matt said, spooning gravy onto his biscuits.

"So do football players," David said, reaching across his twin brother to grab a scone. "Like my Dad. He can really eat, can't he, Grandma?"

"He can indeed."

Langston finally returned, but he ushered in two guests instead of one. Lenora was surprised to see Aidan Jefferies with Melvin.

"Hey, just in time to dig in," Melvin said. "How's that for timing?"

Aidan smiled and planted a kiss on Lenora's cheek. "Hope I'm not intruding. I can wait in the living room until you've finished your meal."

"Nonsense," Lenora answered quickly. "Not only do you have to eat, you have to tell me how delicious everything is."

"Several times," Zach said. "Those who fail to praise excessively never get invited back."

Aidan grinned. "I'm sure I'll love every bite."

Lenora pushed away from the table. "I'll get another plate."

"Keep your seat, Mom," Langston said. "I'm already up."

Melvin tousled the boys' hair and waved to the rest of the family, then grabbed another chair and slid it next to Jaime's.

"Did you two come out together?" Bart asked.

"No," Aidan said. "We just happened to turn in your gate at the same time."

Aidan gave no indication that this was anything other than a chance visit, but Lenora doubted that to be the case. He and Langston were the best of friends and had been for years, but the busy Houston homicide detective seldom showed up unannounced.

Whatever Aidan's reason for coming, he managed to join in the jocular mood of the group as the food disappeared. Melvin kept the conversation interesting by sharing some of the more fascinating accounts of his recent trip. Her granddaughter Gina added excitement when she described her winning performance in the barrel-racing competition at the local rodeo the night before. Fortunately, Lenora had been there to see the feat firsthand.

Thankfully, no one brought up Kali or Louisa Kellogg during the meal. Nonetheless, the situation monopolized Lenora's thoughts. She was almost certain that Aidan had come to talk to them about a development in the murder case and that the news would not be good.

Chapter Three

As soon as the meal was finished, Zach grabbed a cup of coffee and followed Aidan and Langston out to the screened porch that served as a family room much of the year. It was protected from the wind and most winter days that was enough to leave it comfortable.

Today it was downright chilly, but if Aidan had any news about Louisa Kellogg, Zach wanted to hear it firsthand. Thoughts of the homicide had lingered in his mind long after he should have been asleep last night.

"I guess you heard about the murder we had at the Silver Spurs Ranch," Zach said even before Aidan had settled in one of the wooden rockers.

"Yeah. Actually, that's why I'm out this way. I'm going to team up with your local sheriff's department on the investigation."

"Is that standard procedure when the victim's from your jurisdiction?"

"How did you learn the victim was from Houston? The identification of the body is barely official."

Zach perched on the arm of the sofa. "Ed Guerra called late last night and said the body had been identified as Louisa Kellogg and that she was a student at the University of Houston."

"That's accurate. She was a sophomore communications major," Aidan said. "Her parents live in Arizona. They're on their way to Texas now. She was an only child, so I suspect this is going to go down hard with them."

"It would kill me if something like that happened to Gina," Langston said.

Zach was still trying to get a handle on the details. "The Silver Spurs is a long way from Houston. How did Louisa and her killer end up out here?"

"That's one of the unanswered questions. She left the local coffee shop where she worked just after ten o'clock Friday night. That only leaves about two hours between the time she was last seen and the time Kali found the body."

"Did you get the case with the luck of the draw?" Zach asked.

"No. It's possible her murder might be connected to an ongoing case I've been working on."

"Another murder?" Langston asked.

"Not confirmed. Sue Ann Griffin disappeared approximately five months ago from the same area. She hasn't been seen or heard from since."

"And you think the man who killed Louisa Kellogg might have killed the Griffin woman, as well," Zach said.

"It's just a possibility at this point, but that's why I asked to be in on this investigation. I spent a couple of hours with Ed Guerra getting his take on what he found at the Silver Spurs Friday night. Now I plan to make a call on Kali Cooper and see if she'll let me look around."

"Do you think Ed's team missed something?" Langston asked. "They may not be up to Houston standards, but they have one of the most respected Criminal Investigations Divisions in the state."

"It sounds as if they covered all the bases, but I get a better feel for a case when I've visited the crime scene myself. Naturally, I would have liked to be there the night Kali found the body, but this will have to do."

Zach sipped his coffee. "Are you looking for anything in particular at the Silver Spurs?"

"No, but I'm hoping it will hit me if I find it. With luck we'll have fingerprints and DNA on this one. If not, this could be a long, drawn-out process."

"It seems odd that the killer brought his victim all the way out here just to shoot her inside the front door of a deserted ranch house," Zach said. "He could have just dumped her in the woods."

"That's what puzzles me the most," Aidan admitted. "The only thing I can figure at this point is that he chose that particular spot because he knew the ranch was deserted."

Zach didn't buy it. "That's still a long way to drive to put a couple of bullets in a woman's head."

"He likely intended to do more than kill her. There

were no signs of sexual or physical abuse, but that could be because he was interrupted."

"By Kali's arrival," Zach said.

"It's all speculation."

"If the killer knew the place was deserted, he must have ties to this area." Langston said. "He could be someone we know."

That was a possibility Zach had already considered, yet it ground in his stomach all the same. "Mind if I tag along when you go to the Silver Spurs?" he asked, surprising himself with the request.

"Any particular reason?"

"I made a neighborly call on Kali Cooper yesterday at Mother's insistence, just to make sure she was all right. She's jumpy and running on nerves. At least, that was my take. She might be more comfortable with having you look around if you show up with someone she knows."

Aidan smiled for the first time since they'd started talking about the murder. "That wouldn't have anything to do with the fact that she's a very attractive woman now, would it?"

"Who said she's attractive?"

"Ed Guerra. He may be old and married, but he's not dead."

"Kali's looks have nothing to do with my offer," Zach said, stretching the truth a little. "I'm just trying to help."

"In that case, come along. You might just stumble onto the definitive clue."

Doubtful, and Zach had planned on driving into Houston this afternoon to attend a special showing of a new lady friend's work at one of the local galleries—a very beautiful and available lady friend. So why had he just volunteered to go to the Silver Spurs to visit a woman who had thrown him out yesterday?

He let the question ride, mainly because he had no idea how to answer it.

KALI'S MUSCLES tightened and she jerked to attention at the sound of the approaching vehicle. Sheriff Ed Guerra had alerted her that a Houston homicide detective named Aidan Jefferies who was assisting with the case would be paying her a visit. She assumed this was him, but ran for the shotgun anyway.

She was taking no chances. Not that she'd ever fired a shotgun before or even knew for certain this one was loaded correctly. She'd bought it at a pawn shop in Atlanta because one of her friends had convinced her she couldn't live on a ranch without a gun.

Who'd have guessed she would need it so quickly or for such a frightening purpose?

A groan slipped from her lips when she glanced through the open window and saw Zach Collingsworth step from the passenger side of the black sedan. He looked great, of course. But then he hadn't been mopping floors or scrubbing layers of caked dirt from baseboards and window facings.

The rubber gloves came off with a quick jerk. Her hair did not cooperate so well. She didn't recognize the man with Zach. He could be one of Zach's brothers. Might even be the Houston detective Sheriff Guerra had mentioned, though she didn't know why a Houston detective on official duty would be traveling with Zach.

She leaned the shotgun against the front door and stepped onto the porch empty-handed to greet them like a sane person instead of the nervous Nellie she'd become.

"Detective Aidan Jefferies," the man said, speaking first. "I'm with the Houston Police Department. Sheriff Ed Guerra was supposed to call you and tell you I'd be stopping by."

"He did."

"I hate to bother you on a Sunday, but I wanted to take a look around the crime scene as soon as possible. They tend to deteriorate fast."

"I'm afraid this one already has. The sheriff said I was free to clean up the blood and fingerprint powder. But he took multiple pictures before the body was taken to the morgue."

"I saw them, and he was very thorough. I'm probably wasting your time, but I'd still like to ask a few questions and look around."

"Fine by me. Whatever it takes to apprehend the killer."

Zach stamped the mud from his boots, tipped his black Stetson and smiled. Her heart betrayed her, quickening her pulse and skipping a couple of beats.

"We missed you at dinner last night," he said,

stepping closer. "Mom said to extend a rain check, valid any night."

"Thanks. I'll use it soon." She opened the door and the two men followed her inside. "It's a bit chilly in here," she apologized, "but I had to raise a couple of windows to let the strong odors of the cleaning solutions escape."

"No problem," Aidan said, shedding his coat, his gaze already focused on the spot inside the door where she'd found the body.

She stepped back as the gory image reclaimed her mind.

Aidan examined the lock on the front door. "It doesn't look as if it were jimmied."

"No. The attorney gave me keys, but the door was unlocked when I arrived. I don't think my grandfather ever locked it when he was alive. I know he didn't the summer I visited."

"That's not unusual out here," Zach said.

Aidan nodded. "I hope you're keeping it locked now."

"I am, but Sheriff Guerra said the killer would have no reason to return."

"I suspect he's right," Aidan said, "but keeping your doors locked is a good idea in general."

Aidan stepped away from the door. "Can you describe exactly what you heard and saw when you arrived at the Silver Spurs Ranch Friday night?"

"I gave a full statement to Sheriff Guerra. Didn't he show it to you?"

"I read it, but I always like to hear the story from the witness. You may remember something more now that the horror isn't so fresh in your mind."

"I doubt that," she said. "There's nothing to remember. I just walked in, saw the body and let out a scream that probably frightened wildlife for miles."

"A natural reaction," Aidan said. He pulled a pen and small black notebook from his pocket. "Shall we sit?"

"Certainly. Would you like something to drink? I have sodas, and I can make coffee."

"Perhaps later," Aidan said.

She felt the intensity of his stare biting into her. She shifted nervously and dropped to the sofa. Zach sat down beside her, a little too close. The air in the room thickened like clotted cream.

"Just say any and everything that pops into your mind," the detective said, "even if you think it's unimportant. And start at the beginning."

"I saw the rivulets of blood spilling out the door. At first I thought it was paint. Then I opened the door and there was the body." She hesitated as the frightening memories seemed to swell in her mind and press against her temples.

"Before that," Aidan said. "Go back to the point where you first pulled into the gate at the Silver Spurs. Did you see or hear anything that struck you as unusual."

"No…except that when I got out of my Jeep to open the gate, I kind of freaked out for no apparent reason. I attributed it to the isolation. I still think that's what it was, since there was no one around."

"Was it raining at that point?"

"No, but the storm was rolling in and the lightning and thunder had become almost constant. Once I closed the gate and got back in the car, all I thought about was trying to make it to the house before the monsoons started."

"So there was no sign of any other vehicle once you entered the gate?"

"No. I know the sheriff thinks the victim hadn't been dead long, but the killer must have been off the property before I arrived."

"Not necessarily," Zach said. "The main gate is not the only entry."

"It's the only one I know about," Kali said.

"And the only one the sheriff mentioned," Aidan said.

Zach leaned forward. "There's an old logging road that leads to a back gate off Mullins Road. There's no sign on that gate, and the road's not used very often, but it's there. I was on it a couple of years ago when I helped Kali's grandfather haul a load of hay over to Billy Mack's. He was short of hands that summer."

"Interesting," Aidan said as he scribbled notes in the notebook.

"If the killer knew about the back road, he'd have to have some connection with the ranch," Kali said.

"It's a possibility," Aidan agreed, but failed to

elaborate on the point. "Were there any lights on inside the house when you drove up?"

"No. The house was pitch-dark except when—" Her breath caught at the frightening flashback.

"Go ahead," Aidan said.

"It was dark except when the lightning lit up the sky. When I drove up, I thought I saw someone run from the house and into the trees."

Zach turned to face her. "I can't believe you got out of the car when you thought someone might be hiding in the trees."

"I didn't see the shadow again so I thought I was overreacting. But now I realize it could have been the killer. I may have frightened him off. If I'd arrived a few minutes earlier, Louisa Kellogg might still be alive."

"Or the sonofabitch could have killed you, too," Zach said.

"But he didn't," Aidan said. "Let's just deal with what we have."

Kali tried to fight the apprehension that was taking hold again. What they had was a killer who may have seen her. He could have heard her scream, might have sensed her terror. Might know she lived here alone.

"Do you know how to use that shotgun by the door?" Aidan asked, as if reading her fear.

She took a deep breath. "No."

"It's a good time to learn—not only how to shoot a shotgun, but also a pistol, as well."

"I don't own a pistol."

"I have one I can give her," Zach said. "And I can teach her how to use both of them."

"Good idea," Aidan said.

Kali hugged her arms around her chest. "And I thought my problems were over when the judge finally gave me clearance to move out here and take over the ranch."

"Well, I hope we'll make a quick arrest," Aidan said, standing. "In the meantime, Sheriff Guerra will be your go-to man. Now I'd like to take a look around outside."

"Look all you want." She stood and walked to open the front door for him.

"I appreciate that. If I have any other questions, I'll get back to you. And if you think of anything else, call me." He took a business card from his wallet and handed it to her.

Unfortunately Zach didn't exit the house with Aidan. He walked over to join her at the door and placed his hands on her shoulders, massaging her tense muscles. She melted at his touch before abruptly pulling away. She had enough problems without feeding an unreasonable lust for him.

"Sorry," Zach said. "I wasn't trying to get fresh. You just looked stressed to the point of collapse."

"I admit I'm a little frazzled. I wasn't prepared for all of this."

"Then we should go shooting when Aidan finishes up here. Nothing like firing a few rounds to loosen you up."

She was definitely in Texas. "You don't have to

teach me to shoot, Zach. I know you're busy, and I'm sure I can hire someone to—"

He put up a hand to stop her refusal. "You can't hire better than me. I'll show Aidan around and then I can take you back to Jack's Bluff for a lesson."

"Can't we just practice here?"

"We could, but Jack's Bluff has a shooting range already set up. And I have the perfect pistol for you. Lightweight. Easy to use. My sister Jaime has one just like it. She killed a striking copperhead with it last summer when she was horseback-riding with my niece Gina."

Snakes. Killers. Time spent with Zach Collings-worth. Kali didn't even want to think of what other dangers were waiting for her now that she'd moved to the ranch.

"It will give my Mom a chance to say hello, too. You may not remember her after not seeing her for fifteen years, but it's good to know your neighbors out here."

"Then I guess I'll have my lesson at Jack's Bluff."

She watched Zach head outside and then rushed to shower and change clothes. She refused to enter-tain romantic notions about her and Zach Collings-worth, but there was no way she was going to climb in the car with him smelling like bleach.

And if she wore the gorgeous teal sweater she'd splurged on just before leaving Atlanta, well, it just made good sense that she'd want to make a good im-pression on her first visit to a neighboring ranch.

Chapter Four

Learning to fire a pistol was not the way Kali had envisioned spending her first weekend in Texas. In fact, the horrors that had greeted her arrival seemed to be dictating every aspect of her life. The peaceful, pastoral existence she'd dreamed of seemed to be balanced on a bed of hot coals with every step she made holding the potential for disaster.

Sitting in the front seat of a pickup truck and bumping and grinding down a maze of ranch roads with Zach Collingsworth merely switched the danger from an unknown killer to risks of heartache. There was simply no way to be around him and not pick up on his sensual, sexy vibes.

Their eyes met as they turned toward each other at the exact same moment. Kali struggled to breathe as if oxygen were in short supply. She turned away quickly, but couldn't shake the vision of his dark hair spilling from under his Stetson and falling across his forehead, highlighting his chocolate-brown eyes.

Get a grip, girl.

It was a warning she had to heed. She hadn't given up her job and apartment in Atlanta and withdrawn every cent of her savings to get buried in an old schoolgirl crush.

"I enjoyed seeing your mother and sisters again," she said, choosing what should be a safe topic. "I remember Jaime a lot better than I remember Becky, but I don't think I would have recognized either of them. Your Mom looks much the same, though, still as nice and attractive as ever."

"Mom liked you, too. She's never that talkative with people she doesn't like."

"Where was the rest of your family?"

"Probably up at Langston's weekend cabin."

"Oooh. Look. What was that?" Kali asked, as a large olive-and-brown bird that looked as if it was having a bad-hair day raced across the road in front of them and then disappeared into the brush.

Zach laughed at her enthusiasm. "Nothing but your common every-day roadrunner."

"I thought they were just cartoon characters."

"No, they're for real."

"Texas is different from Atlanta in more ways than one."

"Surely you have birds in Atlanta?"

"None that looked like that, at least not in my neighborhood."

"Did you live right in the city?"

"In the suburbs, but there were no wooded roads

like this one, not even at the riding stables. Our trails meandered along a scenic creek at the edge of a park, but there was a shopping center just across the water that spoiled the effect."

"Sounds far too confining for my tastes, not that I don't like the excitement of city life on occasion. But you must have gotten out of town sometimes."

"Not nearly often enough. Mom worked two jobs for most of my life to make ends meet. But somehow she always found the money for my riding lessons. She was pretty terrific."

"I know all about terrific moms. Mine was always there when we needed her. She still is, but she's taken on a whole new persona these days."

"How's that?"

"My grandfather had a stroke last summer and we found out he'd named her as acting CEO of Collingsworth Enterprises should he become unable to fulfill his duties for any reason. It blew our minds, but she jumped right into career mode. She's doing a bang-up job of it—when she's not driving Langston nuts. She loves to focus on what she calls the humanitarian side of the company."

"I would guess that just from talking to her today. She's involved in lots of charities and community events."

"I'm sure she'll do her best to enlist you in some of them."

"I'd like that after I get settled in. So what exactly is Collingsworth Enterprises?"

"The whole kit and caboodle, to put it in our neighbor Billy Mack's vernacular. It includes Jack's Bluff Ranch, Collingsworth Oil and several production-related subsidiaries."

"Sounds impressive."

"That's why I throw it around," he teased. "How is your mom these days?"

Kali was hit by the familiar ache, but she tried to keep it from seeping into her voice. "Mom died of cancer last year."

"I'm sorry."

"Thanks," she said. "It was a tough loss." Kali dropped the subject and hoped Zach would, too. The painful loss made her feel vulnerable and the events of Friday night had already left her feeling defenseless enough.

Zach stopped the car on a gentle incline at a spot where the dirt road disappeared into a sea of yellowed grass and scrubby brush. "Is this the shooting range?" she asked, not sure what she expected, but sure it was more than what looked to be just another pasture—albeit without cows.

"The range is off to your left," Zach said, "just past that cluster of water oaks and sweet gum trees."

She craned her neck for a better view. There was a mound of high grass that rose at least twenty feet, topped by a flat expanse that gave it the appearance of a plateau. In front of that was a cable with hooks. A bull's-eye-type target hung from one of the hooks about midway down the cable. Not as sophisticated as she'd expected on what Sheriff Guerra had mentioned was the second-largest ranch in the state. No one could accuse the Collingsworths of being pretentious.

"The hill stops the bullets?"

"Right," Zach said, shifting into Park, and killing the engine. "That's the backstop to make sure that bullets that are shot here stay here, though there's nothing beyond it but about forty acres of woods."

"I'm guessing someone had to construct the mound since most of the terrain is relatively flat."

"My dad built it years ago so that he could teach his kids to shoot in a safe environment. Unfortunately, he died before I was old enough to handle a gun."

He climbed out of the truck and Kali followed suit, walking to the front fender to get a better look. "Do you always hit the bull's-eye?"

"Not always, but I'm never far from it."

"Well, don't expect that from me," she said. "I can barely see the target much less find it with a bullet."

"I'll pull it closer. That's what the cable's for. Accuracy at close range is what you're looking for anyway—until you take up hunting."

Which would be never.

Zach walked to the back of the truck and opened the large metal toolbox. "Aidan left some police targets here last time we had a little competition going. They should be perfect for our purposes."

He held up his find, and a hard knot settled in her stomach. The targets were tri-folded cardboard cutouts of a man's body with markings for the brain and the heart. Hit the mark, take out a life.

She backed against the truck. "I'm not sure I'm ready for this, Zach."

"You need to be able to protect yourself if you're going to live out here."

"It seems so…so deadly."

"That's the point." Zach shrugged. "But it's up to you."

Up to her, and she'd never had any desire to pull a trigger. Yet she'd gone for that shotgun quickly enough when she'd feared the killer might have returned to the scene of his brutal crime. And what if he had? Or if he hadn't run the other night? Suppose he'd been waiting when she opened the door?

A gust of wind tousled her hair and blew it into her face. She raked the wild strands back and tucked them behind her ears. "Don't guns make you even a little nervous?"

"Only if one's pointed at me. I grew up with firearms. It's just the way it is out here. Not that we have much crime, but a well-placed bullet can stop a copperhead in its tracks or protect a young calf from a predator."

Copperheads and predators. She was definitely starting a new life. This was no time for her to wimp out.

"Okay, Zach. I'll give it a try."

He nodded. "We'll start slow, let you get used to the gun in your hand. Then we'll cover safety and get in a little target practice. Don't expect to master this in one day. You'll need practice to become accurate."

"I hope I'll *never* have to depend on my shooting ability to protect myself."

"Speaking of protection…"

He hesitated, and her nerves grew taut. "Yeah, go on."

He propped a booted foot on the truck's front bumper. "I'm going to say this straight out, Kali, not to frighten you, but just because it's how I feel about it. I don't think you should stay alone on the Silver Spurs until the man who abducted and killed Louisa Kellogg is arrested."

"The sheriff said there's no reason to think he'll come back to the ranch."

"That's a nice, sensible assumption. I wouldn't stake my life on it."

Zach left it at that and walked over to attach the target to the cable. The heels of his boots crushed the dry leaves and rustled the grass. His head was high, and he looked as if he owned the world. He did own his world.

She was the imposter here—a rancher wannabe. But her dream of raising horses had miraculously fallen into her hands when her grandfather had left her the Silver Spurs, and she'd do whatever it took to survive and prosper—even if it meant learning to shoot.

And she'd do it without falling again for Zach Collingsworth—or for any other sexy cowboy who waited in the wings. Ranch first. Romance a distant second.

ZACH SHOULD BE getting ready for a night spent seducing a gorgeous artist. Instead, for some reason he hadn't quite figured out yet, he was sitting on the hood of his truck drinking a beer with Kali and watching the water in the creek pummel the rocks that blocked its path.

"Look at that unusual squirrel," she said. "He's watching us."

"That squirrel is a weasel."

"It's adorable."

"From a distance. Don't try to pet or pick one up. They're not nearly as friendly as they seem once they sense they're cornered or captured."

"He's still cute."

"Didn't you see weasels when you visited your grandfather?"

"Not that I remember."

"How come you never came back after that one summer?"

"My dad and my grandfather had a serious falling out right after that. I don't think they ever spoke to each other again. I'm not sure about that, though, since my parents divorced when I was in eighth grade. Dad got transferred to the West Coast and started a new life. I didn't see him much after that."

But still her grandfather had left her the ranch. There had to be more to that story than she'd said.

"There's a deer," Kali said, pointing to a small white-tailed doe that had stepped into the clearing and was staring at them through soft brown eyes. "She's absolutely regal."

Zach swallowed hard, moved more than he wanted to admit by Kali's reverence for the animal in its unspoiled habitat. She reminded him a bit of the deer. Cautious. Curious. Vulnerable. Sexy—well not the doe, but Kali.

He was definitely attracted to her, but he had the feeling that getting involved with her would lead to complications. He never liked complications or longevity in romantic relationships.

"I can't wait to explore the Silver Spurs on horseback," she said. "I hope I have lots of deer."

"You will." He swatted at a persistent horsefly that had taken a liking to his neck. "Did you know ahead of time that your grandfather was leaving you the ranch?"

"No, I was stunned at the news, but he didn't actually leave it to me outright. The Silver Spurs only becomes fully mine if I live there for a year," she explained. "Otherwise it goes to Hade Carpenter. He's the son of Grandpa Gordy's third wife. I never met her, but her son is an arrogant clod. He's fought my taking possession of the ranch with months of legal haranguing."

"I've run into Hade a time or two over the years," Zach said. "Once when he was in Cutter's Bar trying to pick up one of the local women. Your description of him is a lot more suitable for mixed company than mine would be."

"Another beer or two and I'd tell you what I really think about him," she said. "But not today. It's getting late, and I still have cleaning to do."

Zach shifted for a better look at Kali as he took another swig of his beer. "You don't seem the type," he said, voicing the thought as it popped into his head.

Her eyebrows arched. "The type to drink a beer outside in freezing weather?"

"It's not freezing. The low tonight is only going to be in the low forties. And there's never a bad time for a cold beer."

"Is that why you keep them in a cooler in the back of your truck?"

"Always be prepared."

"A Boy Scout, too."

"Not me. Little League was the extent of my organized participation." He reached over and knocked away a small black bug that had landed in her flyaway auburn hair. The strands felt as soft and silky as they looked. "You don't seem the type to move out to a ranch by yourself," he said, going back to his original statement.

She stretched and leaned back on her elbows, her gaze fixed on the clouds that floated above them. "What type do I seem?"

"The type who'd hook up with a guy right out of college and have a couple of kids, a dog and two hamsters in the suburbs."

"An interesting pigeonhole. But not for this pigeon."

"Horses are your thing, huh?"

"Yeah. Horses. I fell in love with them on my first visit to the Silver Spurs and they've never let me down. They're far easier to bond with than any man I know. They're honest and readable—most of the time."

"You're not one of those weird horse whisperers, are you?"

"I don't whisper," she said, her voice not only rising, but also taking on a defensive edge. "I relate. If that makes me weird, then I'm one of those."

"Don't get bent out of shape. I'm just asking. Jaime dated a guy who claimed to be a whisperer once. The only thing he was whispering that worked was sweet nothings in Jaime's ear. She finally saw through him just about the time I was ready to knock out his lights."

"Zach, the protector. *You* don't seem the type."

"I have my moments. Which brings me back to a statement I made earlier. I don't think it's a good idea for you to stay at the Silver Spurs by yourself."

"So what is it you think I should do, go find any old college grad to hook up with?"

"That's one option. Another might be to hire a wrangler and let him live in the bunkhouse."

"I don't have any livestock to wrangle."

"But you'll be buying horses soon. Just put him on the payroll a few weeks before you actually need him."

She sat up and finished her beer. "This may come as a shock to you, Zach, but not everyone has unlimited funds to work with. I can't afford to hire a cowboy just for his company."

"Then take one of our wranglers for a while. We're not particularly busy on the ranch right now. I've got just the man for you."

"Now you sound like my friend Ellen back in Atlanta. She's always got just the man for me."

"I can beat any offer Ellen can make. Take Jim Bob Harvey, expert wrangler, easygoing and according to my niece Gina, he does a dynamite Britney Spears imitation."

"Now, that's a selling point."

"He can be temporarily yours for the asking."

"I can't just borrow a cowboy like a cup of sugar, Zach."

"Sure you can. He's visiting his brother up in Waco for the weekend, but he'll come roaring in by bedtime. I'll leave word with Bart to send him over to your place in the morning. I'd bring him and introduce him in person, but I have to go in to Collingsworth Oil early tomorrow. I'm in meetings all day."

A nine-to-five job. Hell of a predicament he'd gotten himself into.

"I'm serious, Zach. I can't just take one of your wranglers and even if I could, the bunkhouse isn't ready for occupancy."

"There you go. You've already got a job for him."

"I'm not a charity case."

"Give it a break, Kali. It's the good-neighbor policy, not welfare. It's expected when you live in Colts Run Cross, especially among the ranchers."

He jumped down from the hood of his brother Matt's truck and extended a hand to her. She ignored it.

"I can take care of myself," she insisted again as she slid off the hood on her own.

But her tone had lost some of its conviction. He'd send Jim Bob over to meet her. He'd win her over in no time flat. She might even fall for him. Plenty of the ladies in town had. Jim Bob just never fell back.

Only, something told him Jim Bob might fall for Kali Cooper. That thought settled in Zach's mind like a three-aspirin headache. Maybe Jim Bob wasn't the right man for the job after all. Not that Zach had any sights set on Kali. But there was no use messing up the mind of a good wrangler for a woman Zach had serious doubts would ever stay in Texas.

IT WAS twenty after ten on Sunday evening and Aidan was still at his desk in police headquarters, currently studying copies of the pictures from the Louisa Kellogg crime scene. The earliest he could expect an autopsy report would be late tomorrow, but he was pretty sure from the photographs that the M.E. wouldn't find that Louisa had been brutalized in any way.

So why abduct an attractive young coed just to drive her sixty miles to an isolated ranch house and put two bullets in her head? It didn't add up. Unless she'd been seeing the man and they'd gone there to make out and then gotten into a fight.

Only her roommate was adamant that Louisa

never cheated and her steady boyfriend had an airtight alibi. He'd been with his team, playing varsity basketball at the University of Oklahoma.

Which meant this might well have been a random abduction. If that was the case, there was a strong possibility that Louisa's murder was connected to his original unsolved case. Both victims were students at the University of Houston. Both were attractive. Both had disappeared from the same area. Both of their cars had been found parked and locked at their places of employment.

Not that Louisa and Sue Ann were the only young women who'd gone missing from the Houston area. With a population of over two million within the city limits alone, there were always a number of women who disappeared without a trace. But it was Sue Ann Griffin's disappearance that haunted him the most.

He stared at his hands, half expecting to see traces of her blood glaring back at him. But all he saw was blurred ink blotches from a leaky ballpoint pen and a smear of chocolate from the candy bar he'd eaten an hour or two ago, washing it down with a diet orange drink out of the machine down the hall.

The backs of his eyes started to burn. He needed sleep, especially since he'd only gotten a couple of hours last night. He'd been called out to a murder/suicide on the southeast side. Houston had seen its share of those this year.

He shoved the crime scene pictures back into the manila envelope and carried them to the file cabinet.

He'd just grabbed his jacket and shoved one arm into the sleeve when his cell phone rang.

He checked the caller ID. Zach Collingsworth. What could he want at this time of night?

ZACH WAS in the kitchen alone, his cell phone pressed to his ear while the conversation he'd just had with Ed Guerra replayed in his mind. "Hope I haven't interrupted anything," he said when Aidan answered the phone.

"I was just wrapping up things at my office."

"Kind of late to be working on a Sunday, isn't it?"

"Too late. How did the shooting lessons go?"

"Fair. Kali's never been around firearms and it shows. Merely holding a 9 mm made her nervous. I'm afraid if it came to protecting herself, the intruder would take the gun away from her."

"That happens all too often," Aidan said, "but you have to give the woman credit for having spunk. If she didn't, she wouldn't be staying out on the ranch by herself after being greeted by a corpse."

"Yeah, that's why I'm calling," Zach admitted. "I can't get away from the facts that the killer could be a psycho pervert from around here. And if he is from around here, he likely knows that Kali's living alone on the Silver Spurs."

"Valid points, but Ed Guerra said he'd have one of his deputies keep an eye on the place."

"From a distance," Zach said. "I just talked to him. He's short a man tonight. He has a deputy in the area of the Silver Spurs, but not assigned specifically to guard Kali. He thinks that's adequate, considering there's no reason to expect the killer to return to the scene of the crime."

"And you don't think that's good enough," Aidan said.

"Do you?"

"My professional answer would be that it's extremely unlikely the killer will return to the scene of the crime this soon—if ever. He'll expect the police to be watching for him."

The exact same thing the sheriff had said. Zach should just let it go.

"The problem," Aidan continued, "is that you never know what a psycho will do."

"My point exactly." Which was why Zach couldn't just let it go. Not that he was responsible for Kali. Still, as Jeremiah had said so often before his stroke: A man always knows what's right. A cowboy always does it. Being raised on Jack's Bluff made him cowboy enough.

"So what are you going to do?" Aidan asked.

"The only thing I can do. I'll have to spend the night on Kali's lumpy couch—whether she likes it or not."

Chapter Five

Kali walked through the house, trying to still the apprehension that had been steadily building since sunset. She'd never minded being alone, except for the first few months after her mother's death when the loneliness had been all-consuming.

Stopping near the front window, she stared into the darkness and wondered what kind of advice her mother would offer if she were here now. Run like crazy until the killer was apprehended, or buck up and trust the sheriff and her instincts to keep her safe if the monster returned to the scene of the crime?

Not that it mattered. Kali couldn't leave. That would be just the kind of action Hade Carpenter would use against her to try to get the ranch for himself.

She filled the teakettle with water from the tap and set it on the back element. While it heated, she returned to the bedroom and located the box of magazines that she hadn't had time to unpack. She yanked the sealing tape loose and peeked inside the box. The current issue of the *Eclectic Horseman* stared back at her temptingly. She wasted no time delving between its covers.

By the time the teakettle whistled, her nerves had settled a bit. Nonetheless, she startled when her cell phone vibrated and thumped about on the kitchen table. She grabbed it and answered, noting as she did that the ID said Out of Area.

"Hello, Kali. Welcome to the Silver Spurs."

"Who is this?"

"Someone who's looking forward to meeting you. I'd almost given up on your moving into your newly inherited domicile."

Her hand tightened on the phone. "If you don't say who this is, I'm going to hang up."

"That's not very hospitable, and after I left you such an interesting welcoming gift. I'm sure it led you straight to the county's illustrious sheriff."

Her breath caught in her throat. Oh, God! This couldn't be the killer. He wouldn't have her number. He'd have no reason to call her. He'd—

"I'm sorry about the blood. I guess that was hard to clean up, but you shouldn't have surprised me that way. Louisa and I weren't nearly through with our fun."

Kali broke the connection as the phone tumbled from her fingers and hit the counter with a dull thud. A rush of anger and fear collided inside her and she raced back to the bedroom for the pistol Zach had insisted she bring back with her.

Her fingers wrapped around the cold metal and

her muscles froze. What was she doing? The sick bastard wasn't here. He was most likely back in Houston, reliving the crime in his depraved mind and loving that he'd frightened her.

She had to get a grip. The first order of business would be alerting the deputy guarding her house. The lightweight pistol felt painfully heavy clutched in her clammy hand, yet she carried it with her to the kitchen to retrieve the stakeout deputy's direct number.

By the time she reached the counter her phone was ringing again. Her heart slammed against her chest. "Why are you doing this?" she screamed into the receiver.

"Kali?"

Zach. She sucked in quick gulps of air. "I'm sorry I yelled in your ear. Your timing was horrendous."

"Why? What's happened?"

"I just had a phone call from the killer. I thought you were him calling back."

Zach muttered a curse. "Have you called 911?"

"No, but I was about to call the deputy who's watching my house when your call came in."

"Go ahead and call him, but don't panic when you see headlights in your driveway. It's me. I'm about a minute away. The deputy on duty knows I'm here. I saw him parked just outside your gate and explained that I was visiting."

Relief flooded her senses, followed closely by a new wave of apprehension. "Why are you here this time of the night? Has something else happened?"

"No, I just thought you might sleep better if you had a man around, even if you are too stubborn to admit it."

She looked up as his headlight beams flooded the front windows and swept through the house. She stared at her worn cotton flannel pajamas and ran her fingers through her hair, still slightly damp from the shower.

If there had been any chance he'd found her attractive, that was out the window now. All for the best, she told herself, her furry slippers making scuffling noises as she walked to the door to let him in.

In spite of everything she'd been through in the past few minutes, her heart did a crazy flutter when she saw him standing in the doorway in his coal-colored Stetson. Why couldn't he just once look less than gorgeous?

"You really don't have to do this," she said, probably unconvincingly.

He grinned as his gaze slid over her frumpy pajamas—with snowmen on them, no less.

"The way you answered that phone, you sure sounded like a lady in need of a cowboy to me."

THE DECISION to come to Kali's tonight had been one of the best Zach had made lately. The second-best had been putting that bottle of premium single malt Scotch into his overnight bag. Kali was playing it cool, but it was evident that the phone call had brought the horror of two nights ago back home again.

He found glasses on the shelf above the dishwasher and poured each of them two fingers of the amber liquor while she talked on the phone to the deputy who was on duty.

"He didn't seem all that surprised by the call," she said, "but he didn't think it was necessarily the killer. Apparently there are crazies who get their rocks off by reading about crimes and then inserting themselves into the havoc."

"I've heard that," he said, but that didn't necessarily mean tonight's caller was one of them. "Try this," he said, handing her the glass.

She sniffed it. "I don't care for hard liquor."

"It will relax you," he said, tapping his glass with hers.

"In that case, I may need another." She dropped to one of the straightbacked chairs that sat around the rectangular wooden table. Zach took the chair on the end, catty-corner from hers. His gaze moved to her face. It looked freshly scrubbed and incredibly soft.

She sipped the drink. "It could have been Hade Carpenter. He has my phone number," she said. "And he'd be mean enough to call just to frighten me."

"Wouldn't you recognize his voice?"

"Not necessarily. I've only spoken to him on a couple of occasions and that was in the lawyer's office. Other than that, my attorney handled everything. The only time Hade called me directly was right after the last judge refused another appeal and said the will was legal and the ranch was mine."

"I'm guessing Hade didn't call to congratulate you."

"Hardly. He said if I thought this was over, I was mistaken. He'd see that I didn't spend a year on the land, and he'd be watching every second so that I couldn't lie about it."

"Where does this charmer live?"

"Cincinnati, and my caller ID said Out of Area, so it could have been him."

"Not likely he'd have heard about the murder up there."

"Knowing him, he probably has spies in the area." She took another sip of the scotch.

A pinpoint of liquid clung to her bottom lip, and Zach found himself staring at it. She had great lips. Full. Not pouty or hesitant to show emotion, but straightforward like the rest of her.

"Tell me more about Hade Carpenter," he said, in an attempt to keep his mind on track.

"Like what?"

"How old is he?"

"Mid-fifties, I think. Most of what I know about him came from my attorney."

"Is your attorney the same one who drew up the will?"

"No, I hired an Atlanta attorney. My grandfather's lawyer was Collin Connelly. Have you heard of him?"

"As a matter of fact, I have. He lives in Colts Run Cross. I've never had legal dealings with him, though. Can you explain the terms of the will in more detail?"

"I can try. The little cash Grandpa had left after his medical bills went to Hade. The ranch went to me if I lived on it for a year. If not, ownership of the ranch and all structures thereon transfer to Hade."

"Sounds clear-cut to me. I can't believe he had the gall to fight that in court?"

"For months."

"Did your grandfather have other grandchildren?"

"No. My dad was an only child and I was *his* only child."

"I can't imagine what that would be like."

"Believe me it's not what it's cracked up to be. Consider yourself lucky to be part of a big family."

"I do. My brothers and I have been known to argue like Texas politicians up for the same office, but I'd put my life on the line for any of them and never give it a second thought. Same for my sister Becky and her boys."

"And Jaime?"

Jaime. His feelings for her were never totally clear even to him. It was the twin thing, he guessed, but he felt more protective of her, almost as if sharing the womb tied them for life with some invisible bond that could be felt but never seen. He'd never even talked about it with her. It was just there. "Same with Jaime," he said.

Zach wasn't convinced the call was from Hade or from any other scare-tactic fake. Who was to say the killer wasn't depraved enough to make the call? Or that he wasn't brazen enough to return to the ranch? If nothing else, the call made an excellent argument for why Kali shouldn't stay at the ranch alone.

"I've talked to Jim Bob," he said. "He's taking up residence here first thing tomorrow morning. I'll stay until he arrives, but then I'll have to go into Houston."

"That's really not necessary, Zach. I—"

"Let it go," he said. "I'm as stubborn as you are. Besides, you can use the help getting this ranch up and running again. I'm sure the stable needs work before you bring in horses, not to mention all the fences that need repairing."

"I *could* use some help. But, I'll pay you for Jim Bob's time. You can bill me for the going rate, but I can't afford to keep him here more than a few days."

"That's the other thing. If you need some funds to get started, I can back you—or sign for you at the bank," he added when he saw the refusal already forming on her lips.

"Thanks, but I don't want to take on any debt if I can help it. I have some savings. I'm hoping it will be enough to get me by until I start making money."

"Just an offer—always available if you happen to change your mind."

She propped her elbows on the table and cradled her face between her hands. Either the liquor was already taking effect or the stress of the day was getting to her.

"You look tired," he said.

"My body's still on Atlanta time, and I haven't slept much the last two nights."

"Then why don't you go to bed? I'll make myself comfortable."

"The guest room's a mess. You take my room, Zach. I'll grab one of the pillows and sleep on the sofa."

"We could share," he teased.

Her mouth opened slightly and a slow burn spread from a tinge to a coat of crimson that covered her cheeks.

"Just kidding," he said quickly. "I threw a sleeping bag in the car. I'll get it and sack out on the sofa."

Her blush was slow in disappearing. "I think I will go to bed," she said. She picked up the two empty glasses and carried them to the sink, rinsing them before placing them in the dishwasher.

Zach watched her, his thoughts going places he'd rather they didn't. Like the way the cute snowmen on her pajamas seemed to be hugging her bottom. She had a very nice behind. Nice breasts, too. Perky enough to peak like nipply mounds of snow for her cuddly snowmen.

His body tightened, and he pushed away from the table and stood. "Guess I'll get that sleeping bag." He started to the door.

"Zach."

Her voice was tentative. He turned, wondering if the fear was taking hold again.

"Thanks for coming over tonight."

"My pleasure." Oddly enough, he meant that, even though he'd be sprawled on a lumpy couch that was probably a half foot too short to accommodate him. Sleeping alone, with an attractive woman only steps away. That in itself was probably a first for him.

He was thankful it was only for one night. No reason to ruin his reputation.

KALI WOKE to the early morning rays of sunshine that spilled though the windows and painted blocks of light across the worn but now spotless and citrus-scented quilt. She rubbed her eyes, adjusting slowly to the unfamiliar surroundings.

It was the first decent sleep she'd had since arriving at the ranch and her body and mind seemed almost numb. But not so out of it that she wasn't keenly aware that Zach Collingsworth was sleeping on a sofa just down the narrow hall.

Stretching, she let her gaze move across the room, taking in every quaint but rustic detail. The old iron bed with the graceful swirls in the footboard. The antique dresser topped by a mirror with wavy lines that elongated her face and made her lips look clown-like. The picture of an Indian in full-dress feathers and a bare chest splashed with war paint that hung on the far wall. A huge pottery urn that served as the base for her bedside table.

She stretched and groaned as nagging aches and pains attacked her shoulders, arms and thighs. All that cleaning combined with too much stress, she decided, as she threw her legs over the side of the bed. The odor of brewing coffee wafted under her closed door.

Obviously Zach had beaten her up.

She wiggled out of her pajama bottoms and un-buttoned the top, shuffling to the closet for clean jeans and a sweatshirt. Once dressed, she grabbed a brush and worked it through the tangled mass of disheveled hair. The tube of lipstick she'd left on top of the dresser seemed to be staring at her and daring her to go for some lightweight glamour. She picked it up then opened the top drawer and dropped it inside with the rest of the makeup she seldom used. Lipstick might give Zach the impression she was interested in more than friendship—which she refused to be.

Disgruntled with herself for giving this much thought to walking to her own kitchen, she headed for the one bathroom—which was down the hall— to splash her face with cold water, brush her teeth and take care of business.

By the time she reached the kitchen, Zach was standing over the range arranging slices of the bacon she'd brought in Colts Run Cross into a sizzling skillet. He was in jeans, but barefoot, his hair uncombed, his shirt unbuttoned and revealing the most decidedly masculine chest she'd ever seen.

He reminded her of a Greek god, if Greek gods had come with a cowboy mystique.

"And you cook, too," she said, managing to keep her tone light.

"On rare occasions."

"Lucky me."

"Better wait until you taste it before you go out on a limb. My breakfasts are nowhere near as good as Juanita's. She's probably frying fresh tortillas for a spicy *migas* about now."

"Okay, two questions," she said, as she poured fresh-brewed coffee into a maroon-colored pottery mug. "Who's Juanita and what's *migas?*"

"*Migas* is a Mexican breakfast item. Eggs, chorizo, corn tortilla pieces, all tangled together with peppers and spices and topped with cheese and salsa—and sometimes avocado."

"That's out for today," she said. "I think eggs might be the only ingredient on hand. So what about Juanita?"

"She's our cook and probably the best one north of the Rio Grande. But never even hint at that fact in front of my mother. She'd fire her on the spot."

"What's wrong with your mother's cooking?"

"Not a thing. Nothing wrong with being second-best north of the Rio Grande. Mom just wouldn't see it quite that way. Not that she has much time for cooking now that's she's acting CEO."

The Collingsworth wealth and influence was mind-boggling to Kali. More amazing was the fact that a man from that kind of background had slept on her lumpy sofa last night and was cooking her breakfast in his bare feet.

"I'll do the eggs," she said. "How do you take yours—other than in spicy concoctions perfected by Juanita?"

"Over easy."

She buttered four slices of bread and slid them into the toaster oven before breaking eggs into a hot skillet. In Atlanta she'd have stopped in the down-town deli for a bagel and eaten it at her desk while going through the morning's e-mail. On good days she finished the bagel and the e-mail before her boss arrived and started barking orders.

Her phone rang. Ed Guerra. At seven in the morning. Apprehension skittered and scratched along her nerves like a startled kitten. She took the call. "Tell me this is good news."

"I wish I could, Kali. I really wish I could, but Chester Maxwell, you know he's the deputy who was keeping an eye on your place last night?"

"I know. What about him?"

"He came across a bloodstained man's shirt layin' in the pine straw near your back gate. We think it could belong to Louisa Kellogg's killer."

She didn't understand the sheriff's concern. "Wouldn't additional evidence be good news?"

"It would be, if that were all he found."

"What else was there?"

"There was a newspaper clipping in the shirt pocket. The article was from the Colts Run Cross newspaper months ago and was about you inheriting the ranch."

"They wrote about that in the newspaper?"

"Colts Run Cross is a small town, Kali. The paper only comes out twice a week, and sometimes something as significant as a Boy Scout getting a merit badge makes the copy. But there's more."

She had a sickening hunch that the worst was yet to come. "Just say it, Sheriff. I'd rather hear it all at once then deal with the dread."

"There was a picture of you in the pocket, too. It

was kind of grainy as if he might have gotten it off the Internet and just printed it out. Your hair was shorter, but it was definitely you."

Probably from her one venture into the world of myspace.com. "Why would he have my picture?"

"I don't know, but it shows that he's familiar with the ranch and the fact that you were inheriting it. His murderous visit to the Silver Spurs wasn't just a chance occurrence."

She sank to a chair, her stomach churning so that breakfast was no longer a viable option. Her dream life had turned into a nightmare and the horrors might be only beginning.

Chapter Six

The latest development created a situation which both puzzled and worried Zach. Assuming the bloodstained shirt belonged to the killer—a fact which they could ascertain from DNA testing—then why had the article and the photo of Kali been in his pocket?

Had he merely read about the inheritance and looked up the information on Kali, or were his ties more personal? As far as Zach could see, neither scenario boded well for Kali's safety. He'd made it clear to Jim Bob that his main focus was to be on keeping Kali safe. Zach wasn't sure even that was enough.

He walked from the parking garage through the entrance of the impressive skyscraper and took the elevator to the eighteenth floor, home to the executive offices of Collingsworth Oil. Two men in dark-blue suits, carrying briefcases and with facial expressions that made Zach think of executioners, rode up with him.

They followed him through the double glass doors across from the elevator and stopped at the receptionist's desk. A surge of irritation shot through Zach as he heard Lottie tell them that Langston was expecting them. He'd hoped to talk to Langston before his own meeting with the government regulators and Melvin got under way.

If all Langston had for him to do was sit around and listen to Melvin negotiate all day, he'd rather drive back to the Silver Spurs and see what needed to be done to make the ranch house more secure.

He was willing to give the job at Collingsworth Oil his best shot this time, but he could do that just as well starting next week. And if it were going to work, he'd need something to sink his teeth into that required more investigative skills. That had always been his strong suit.

Even that might not cut it for him. In spite of being raised on equal parts ranching and oil empire, neither of them really revved his motor, at least not the way they did his brothers.

The secretary assigned him by Langston was a middle-aged woman named Emilie Watson, who usually looked as if she'd just swallowed a persimmon. Most of the time when he was talking to her, she stared at him over the top of her glasses as if she were the teacher and he was a troublesome student. She was on the phone when he approached, but hung up before he reached her desk.

"Good morning, Zach."

"Right back at you. Do you know if Melvin's in yet?"

"No, but I'll check. And Langston wants to see you in his office immediately."

"Are you sure? I just heard Lottie tell a couple of men that he was ready to see them."

"They're from the CIA. He wants you in on the dialogue with them."

"Really? The CIA?"

"That's what I was told."

"Did Langston say how long he expected the dialogue to last?"

"No, but he told me to let Melvin know that he should start the meeting with the government regulators without you. I doubt Melvin will like that. He said you needed exposure to that aspect of Collingsworth Oil."

"Wow, I must be good if the company's two top dogs are fighting over me."

Emilie smiled in spite of herself as she pushed the glasses back up her peaked nose.

"If I get any calls from Kali Cooper or Jim Bob Harvey, forward them to me immediately."

"You'll be with the CIA."

"Yes, and I'll bow and scrape appropriately. But I still want you to forward the calls. The CIA will survive the distraction."

"If that's what you want."

"That's what I insist on."

He smiled but her scolding stare failed to soften.

He didn't bother stopping at his desk, but walked straight to Langston's office.

"Great suit," Langston's secretary said, looking up from her computer monitor. "Makes you reek of power."

"Thanks. Do you think I should ask for a raise?"

"I'd work a full month first," she said, flashing a contagious smile. "The meeting is already underway, but you can join them in progress."

Zach propped two hands on the front corner of her desk. "Want to fill me in on what it's about?"

"Langston wasn't sure, but the last time the CIA called on him they suggested that Collingsworth Oil was involved in funding terrorist activity."

"You have got to be kidding."

"No. Langston assured them the idea was absurd and they left. That was months ago, so this could be an entirely different issue."

"Let's hope, but I'm sure Langston must have looked into the allegations."

"I'm certain he did, but I never heard that there was any substance to them."

Zach opened the door and stepped inside the office and into a shroud of tension so concentrated it felt like the air might explode. Houston, we have a problem.

The two CIA men turned their attention to Zach as Langston made the introductions. The older agent, Tom, put out a hand. His grip was firm. The younger agent, Ralph, did the same and managed an unconvincing smile that suggested he had spent a couple of hours too long with tooth-brightening strips.

It took less than a dozen sentences for Langston to bring Zach up to speed. The agents claimed they had received information from a knowledgeable source that someone with ties to Collingsworth Oil had given money to a high-ranking member of a terrorist group in Saudi Arabia. As before, the man from Collingsworth Oil accused of making the transfer had not been identified, but was reportedly one of the higher-ups in the company.

Zach seriously doubted the authenticity of the claims. Langston ran a tight ship. He was big on ethics and expected the same of his employees and he never hired anyone to a position of responsibility without thorough background checks.

"So, just to clarify," Zach interjected, "all you have at this point is unfounded allegations."

"Very serious allegations," Tom said. "We expect full cooperation from you in finding out if funds have been diverted from Collingsworth Oil to any known terrorist group."

"What they want is carte blanche permission to confiscate our records and share that information with anyone they deem appropriate."

Ralph crossed an ankle over his knee. "If you have nothing to hide, that shouldn't be an issue."

"It is not in Collingsworth Oil's best interest to turn over every aspect of our business dealings to anyone without good cause."

Ralph's brows arched. "And you don't consider fighting terrorism a good cause?"

"I didn't say that. I don't consider unfounded rumors a just reason for disclosure of information to any and everyone you might decide to share it with. This is a very competitive business. Information from our research findings about possible new drilling prospects, pending mergers, etc. can easily be used against us if it falls into the wrong hands."

Tom drummed his fingers on the arm of the chair. "It would be a lot better for you to cooperate with us than to force us to get legal warrants."

"If you had enough concrete evidence to do that, you wouldn't be asking for my cooperation," Langston said. "You'd be making arrests. Which is exactly where you were the last time you sent agents to see me. If there was any basis to your allegations, I'd think you'd have proof by now or at least a name you could give me."

"I'm sorry you feel that way, Mr. Collingsworth, but I can assure you that arrests are forthcoming with or without your cooperation."

"You mean if the allegations are verified, don't you?" Zach said.

"Well, yes, of course that's what I meant."

"Well, you see it's like this," Langston said. "If one red cent of Collingsworth Oil money has gone to terrorism or any crime against this country, it was without my knowledge. If you give me a name, I'll get to the bottom of this immediately."

"Since you refuse to do that, it may take me longer to identify the culprit—if there is a culprit. But rest assured that if I discover any ties between one of my employees and terrorists, I will turn him over to you so fast that if he's brushing his teeth he won't have time to rinse."

"We're equipped to handle this much more efficiently than you are," Ralph assured him.

Zach smiled. "I wouldn't bet on that."

"We have the resources of the government at our disposal."

"And we all know how efficient the government is," Langston quipped, though Zach knew he was not taking these accusations lightly. His muscles were flexed as if he was gearing up for a fight. If someone had crossed the line, Langston would discover it.

Tom ran his tongue over his back teeth as if trying to loosen a sesame seed. "I was really hoping we could handle this in a friendly way."

"We are," Langston assured him. "As I told the last agents who were here a few months back, I attended the Air Force Academy and spent four years on active duty. My father died while serving in the Air National Guard. I support what you're doing wholeheartedly. It's your methods as they pertain to Collingsworth Oil I disagree with."

"It seems this would go more efficiently for everyone if you'd identify the employee you suspect," Zach said.

"We're not at liberty to do that."

Langston tented his hands and leaned back in his leather chair. "Then I guess that leaves us at a standoff."

The meeting ended pretty quickly after that, and it was clear the agents were not pleased by the outcome. Still, they managed a halfway friendly exit.

"You don't really think there's anything to those allegations, do you?" Zach asked when the door had closed behind them.

"I didn't the last time the CIA was here, and a full in-house investigation didn't produce any evidence. But since they're back I'm starting to believe they might be on to something. In spite of our intense screening, I guess a traitor could have found his—or her—way into the executive ranks."

"So what will you do?"

"Conduct another full investigation and this time I'll hire outside experts. If I find out that someone in this organization cooperated in any way with a terrorist group, I'll be thrilled to turn him over to the CIA. You know how strongly I feel about the security of our country."

"I know. I'm just not sure the CIA duet who just left here picked up on that. Anyway, I was surprised you wanted me in on the meeting."

"Why? You work here now and you're family. Accusations like that affect all of us."

"I realize that," Zach said, "but thought maybe you were just urging me to come back to work because Mother is adamant that I get started on some kind of career."

"Actually, I like having you on board and you have a lot to offer the company. You just have to find your niche."

Zach had trouble thinking of himself settled into a niche, but this wasn't the time to get into that. He decided to discuss what was really on his mind.

Zach updated Langston on the latest developments in the murder case, fighting the anger as he talked about the article and photo found in the pocket of what was likely the killer's shirt.

"That definitely ups the danger level," Langston said. "Is Kali Cooper alone on the ranch now?"

"Jim Bob is staying with her today. Bart said he could spare him as long as she needed him to help in any way he could, but he's not a bodyguard."

"No, but he's level-headed and dependable. And a damn good shot. I'd stack him up against most paid protectors."

"Good points."

Langston shrugged out of his suit jacket and draped it across the back of his chair. He was dressed to the nines, but still in his cowboy boots. You can take the man off the ranch, but you can't take the ranch out of the man.

"How is Kali holding up?" Langston asked.

"A hell of a lot better than I would have expected considering the situation. She was upset when I got there last night, but that was right after the threatening phone call. She settled down fairly quickly. Still I think she was relieved that I was sleeping over."

"Whoa. Did you just say you spent the night with Kali Cooper? That's moving a little fast even for you, isn't it?"

"It would be if it was as interesting as you make it sound. I slept on the sofa—alone. It seemed the neighborly thing to do."

"I thought the sheriff was having a deputy watch her place."

"He had a deputy in the area. He wasn't assigned strictly to Kali. Besides, Colts Run Cross deputies aren't exactly used to dealing with psycho killers."

"Then your interest in Kali is all about protection?"

"Would it matter if it wasn't?"

"She's vulnerable right now and if she falls for you, it could mean trouble. Neighbor romances are a lot like office affairs. When the romance dies, the other person is still there, and it's almost always uncomfortable if not downright miserable for somebody."

Definitely not the type of situation Zach was looking for. "You sound as if you've been there."

"Not in a long, long time."

And likely never again. Both Langston and his brother Bart were like walking advertisements for marriage and happy ever after.

"You might give Aidan a call and see what he thinks of the latest developments at the Silver Spurs," Langston said. "He'll level with you if he thinks Kali needs paid protection."

"Good idea. If this is all you have for me now, I guess I should get back to Melvin's meeting," Zach said.

"Right. You can learn a lot from Melvin. And keep me posted on the murder case."

"Will do."

By the time Zach reached Melvin's office, the few facts he knew about the murder were running rough-shod through his mind. The good thing about knowing the killer might have direct ties to the ranch was that it should give Aidan and Ed Guerra some-where to start. The bad thing was that it meant looking at everyone who'd ever worked for or had been in close contact with Gordon Cooper. Wran-glers, relatives, neighbors, business associates, friends. The possibilities were endless.

A name sprang to Zach's mind and flashed like neon. He spun around and headed back to his own office. Melvin didn't really need him. Aidan Jeffer-ies just might.

"MAN, this place looks like a hurricane came through and then backed up for another shot," Jim Bob said as he followed Kali into the stable. "You might be better off just tearing it down and building a new one."

"I was thinking I could make necessary repairs and then later build a newer and a more modern struc-ture after I have an income."

"That'll probably work, too. What kind of horses are you going to put in here?"

"I know it sounds ambitious, but I want to breed and raise quarter horses."

"Ambition's a good thing, I guess. I'm pretty much satisfied as a plain old cowboy right now, but I might want my own spread one day."

"What's it like working for the Collingsworths?"

"Like working for a second family. They treat me well. Plus they run the ranch right. Even though they're all about business, the animals get the best of care."

"That's what I want for my horses—the best of care." Kali stepped over a hayfork that had fallen across the narrow path between the stalls. "I'm thinking I can board and train horses for other people as well. There must be a lot of Houston residents who'd love to own horses and ride regularly if they had somewhere to keep them and I could do the work for them."

"They might. I know Langston's daughter Gina can't wait to get out here every weekend and straddle a saddle."

Jim Bob swung open the creaky door to one of the stalls. A giant, hairy spider dropped from the wooden slats and crawled across the hay in Kali's direction. She jumped back, almost tripping over a ceiling joist that had come loose and swung haphazardly from the roof.

"He ain't gonna hurt you," Jim Bob said, smiling broadly.

"How can you be so sure?"

"There's only two kinds of spiders you have to worry about in Texas and that wasn't one of them. It just looks mean."

"Which two should I worry about?"

"The black widow and the brown recluse are both

venomous. If they bite you, you'll know it, though it won't likely kill you. But most of the time you leave them alone, and they'll do the same for you."

"Spiders, rattlesnakes and cold-blooded killers. Anything else I should worry about?"

"Occasionally you might run across a scorpion. I'd stay clear of them, as well."

Kali planned to. She stared up at a wide strip of sunlight that poured through a huge hole in the roof. "I guess I'm lucky the roof hasn't blown off altogether."

"Yep. Billy Mack lost a barn to a tornado last year. Crazy storm just fell out of the sky in that one spot and made splinters of the thing. But don't worry about that, either," he said, obviously noting her look of dismay. "We don't get all that many tornados down here. A hurricane spawned that one."

"Hurricanes and tornados. Tell you what, Jim Bob, how about not trying to make me feel better for the rest of the day?"

He grinned, and the mischievous tilt of his lips made him look even younger, though there was a hint of seriousness about him still. It was the situation, she decided. The recent murder spread its dark shroud over everything and everyone.

"I'll start on the repairs as soon as I clean out the bunkhouse, providing you stick around and watch so I can do my protective bit."

His willingness to jump in with the work surprised her, but…"I can't let you do that."

He nudged his Western hat back a bit and scratched his head. "How come?"

"You're a wrangler, not a handyman."

"You do have a lot to learn about ranching. The job description for wrangler is pretty much, you do what needs doing."

"Including getting stuck protecting neighboring women ranchers?"

"Nope." He kicked at a mound of hay in the corner of the stall, stirring up a cloud of dust as well. "Hanging out over here is a perk. You're a dang sight prettier than a Brahma."

"You sure talk kindly, cowboy," she teased.

He grinned and kept on nosing about the empty stall, as if he expected to find treasure buried in the hay.

He did have the look of a traditional cowboy. Young, with dark curly hair on the scraggly side that crawled inside the collar of his jacket. And she was certain he had the bluest eyes she'd ever seen. Her friend Kate would go nuts over him.

And still he was plain vanilla compared to Zach—not that she was comparing or even thinking about Zach.

"How long have you worked for the Collingsworths?" she asked when he exited that stall and stepped inside another.

"Four years. I came to work for them right after I graduated high school. The first two years I only worked to get money to pay the entrance fees into every rodeo within a day's drive."

"What made you give that up—or have you?"

"Gave it up a year and a half ago. The credit goes to a very mean bull named Disaster. He broke both my legs and a rib. Decided after that I was better suited to punching cows." He stooped to pick up a saddle blanket that had been tossed into a corner and left to rot.

"What are you looking for?" she asked.

"Nothing in particular. When the sheriff was here, he told me to keep a lookout for anything unusual. I'm just following orders."

But he was being too thorough. "You think the killer may have been in here at some point, don't you?"

"What would I know about that? Sheriff Guerra and Aidan Jefferies are the experts."

Still, just thinking that the killer might have hung out in the stable, that he might have lurked around the ranch in the weeks that it had been deserted sent icy chills up her spine.

She was still letting her mind dip into the macabre possibilities when her phone rang. This time the number was one she recognized. It was Kate. With any luck, she hadn't heard the bad news. Kali hated the thought of answering a new multitude of questions about the gore that had become her reality.

"Hi, Kate, what's up?" she asked, keeping her voice as upbeat as possible.

"Just checking to see if ranch life is as exciting as you'd imagined it would be."

"Oh, it's exciting, all right."

"Great. I can't wait until I get some time off so I can come down."

"You know you're always welcome."

"And I have a quick question for you," Kate added.

"Shoot."

"Prissy is still giving me fits. She's fine while I unfasten the throat latch and cavesson, but when I try to take the bridle off over her ears, she gets so nervous I have trouble controlling her."

Kate had just bought her first horse and fretted worse than a new mother, but Kali could tell this was more than just the jitters. "Did you talk to someone at the stables about the problem?"

"I thought I'd ask you first."

"Does it upset Prissy when you put the bridle on?"

"No, just when I take it off. It's a bad scene. So how do I show her who's boss?"

"First, don't think of it as a power struggle. She's trying to tell you something, and you have to figure out what that something is."

"And just how do I do that?"

"Make sure you aren't hurting her ears when you remove the bridle, and remove it one ear at a time. Stand just—" Kali stopped mid sentence, her concentration focused solely on what Jim Bob was pulling from beneath a pile of hay.

Apprehension started in the pit of her stomach and spread to burn in her chest. "Something's come up," she said. "I'll have to call you back."

"What's wrong?"

Kali broke the connection without responding to the question. "That's a woman's skirt," she said, stating the obvious in a scratchy voice. It was sliced from the waist to the hem in several spots and stained with what looked to be blood.

"It must have belonged to the victim," Jim Bob said. "I'll call the sheriff."

"The victim was fully clothed when I found her."

"Then it's probably nothing," he said, already punching numbers on his cell phone.

It was a long way from nothing. Could the skirt belong to another victim? Was her ranch a killer's lair?

Her blood ran cold as a terrifying premonition swept her mind reaching icy fingers to her soul. The killer wasn't through with Silver Spurs...or with her.

Chapter Seven

Zach met Aidan at a hole-in-the-wall café just off I-610 West. They ordered two large black coffees and a half dozen glazed donuts, taking them back to Aidan's unmarked police car so that they could talk in private. Aidan released the catch and eased his seat back as far as it would go before biting into the sugary chunk of carbs and calories.

Zach sipped his coffee, but shook his head when Aidan pushed the sack of donuts his way. He had a serious lack of appetite today. As he'd suspected, Aidan had already heard about the shirt found on the Silver Spurs this morning.

Aidan chewed and swallowed. "So what's on your mind that you didn't want to talk about over the phone?"

"I was thinking about the Silver Spurs murder and how the culprit was most likely familiar with the ranch, and I came up with a name you might want to check out."

"Someone you think might have killed Louisa Kellogg?"

"A long shot."

"Any shot would be good at this point."

Static-laced chatter boomed from the police radio. There had been an armed robbery of a neighborhood grocery store in southeast Houston. The suspect was being chased by two cops on foot who wanted backup. Aidan listened then lowered the volume.

"Do you need to respond to that?" Zach asked.

"No. There are plenty of cops in that area. They'll be on the scene long before I could get there. So who's the guy you're thinking could be the perp?"

"Tony Pinter. Have you ever heard of him?"

"Not that I recall. What's his claim to fame?"

"He was Gordon Cooper's foreman. He had a personality like a Doberman who hadn't eaten in days."

"So why did Gordon keep him around?"

"I suspect he knew his stuff when it came to livestock. Good foremen are hard to come by these days. And oddly enough he and Gordon seemed to get along. Some people around Colts Run Cross even speculated that Gordon might leave him the ranch."

"Interesting. Do you have any idea where this Tony Pinter is now?"

"Not a clue. Jeremiah would," Zach said, "if he was himself." Before the stroke his grandfather had been sharp as a tack and could have told them anything they wanted to know about all the neighboring ranchers and their foremen. Now it was a crap shoot as to whether or not he'd even recognize all of the family.

"I may run out to see him anyway," Aidan said. "If I don't get anywhere with him, I can always try Billy Mack. He seems to keep track of everybody."

"Right. Don't know why I didn't think of him first." Zach stretched his legs as much as the space would allow. "Have you got anything on Hade Carpenter yet?"

Aidan nodded as he finished the donut and wiped his mouth on one of the thin paper napkins. "He doesn't have any outstanding warrants against him or any convictions, but he's been arrested several times over the past few years."

"What were the charges?"

"DUI, threatening a neighbor with a baseball bat, and spousal abuse, one time so severe that his wife ended up in the hospital with a broken arm. She was six months pregnant at the time."

"Nice guy," Zach said, wondering how rotten—or how high—a man would have to be to pull a stunt like that. "Why didn't he do jail time?"

"He got out of the DUI charges with fines and community service. The neighbor didn't show up on the court date and his wife withdrew the charges.

"That's the way more often than not in spousal abuse cases. Unless the abused partner is committed to getting out of the marriage they usually drop charges. Fortunately for Hade's wife, she finally divorced him."

"So he's single now?"

"Yeah, he lives alone in an apartment complex in a Cincinnati suburb, at least he did until a week ago."

"What happened then?"

"The apartment manager said he moved out without giving the required thirty-day notice. He told her he'd inherited a ranch in Texas."

Zach muttered a few well-chosen curse words. "What do you think he meant by that?"

"Maybe he thinks Kali won't last long at the Silver Spurs."

"Especially if he leaves her a body as a house-warming gift. Only it's hard to believe a man would kill someone for that little, rundown spread."

"People have killed for far less," Aidan said, "though I doubt it happened in this case. There are much easier and less self-defeating ways to frighten someone than murder."

"But *someone* killed Louisa Kellogg," Zach said, "and chances are damn good that whoever did was also carrying around that article about Kali. How soon will we know if that was Louisa's blood on the shirt?"

"I've requested a rush on the DNA, but it still depends on how backed up the lab is. We could know as early as tomorrow—or as late as the end of the week."

"I'd appreciate it if you'd let me know when you hear something."

"Sure." Aidan tossed the bag with the remaining

donuts to the back seat of the car then turned back to Zach. "You ever think of becoming a detective?"

"Can't say that I have."

"Maybe you should. You'd be good at it."

Zach seriously doubted that. He wasn't fond of killers or long hours, and he knew Aidan pretty much lived with both. His phone vibrated and he reached into his pocket for it. A disturbing mix of apprehension and anticipation surfaced as he checked the caller ID. "Hi, Kali."

A moment later the mix changed to unadulterated dread.

AIDAN REVVED the engine of his unmarked car as Zach walked away. His mind was working overtime, details of the previous disappearance haunting him the way they had so many nights over the past year. Only that time he'd known the victim. He'd been in the pizza restaurant where she'd worked that very night, had flirted with her when she'd brought his pepperoni combo to the table, even been flattered when she'd scribbled her phone number on his receipt.

She'd never made it home that night. The same way Louisa Kellogg had never made it home on Friday night. Both of them working late in a neighborhood establishment, both students at U of H, neither having any known enemies. Both exceptionally pretty. Now Aidan had to wonder if the blood on the skirt found in the long-deserted stable at Silver Spurs could belong to Sue Ann.

The only thing he was certain of at this point was that Louisa Kellogg was dead and Kali Cooper was most likely in danger. And that Zach Collingsworth had taken a very unexpected interest in the case.

He liked Zach, always had, even envied him at times. The guy had beautiful women lined up as if he were a rock star. It was just that jumping into a murder case wasn't his style. Could it be that he'd actually fallen for Kali and this was the real thing?

Not likely. He'd been playing the field too long. Still Aidan was grateful for the lead Zach had given him. He'd put someone on Tony Pinter right away. He already had someone tracking down the whereabouts of Hade Carpenter. He made the call to the station, then shoved his emergency light into place and took I-610 to the Hardy Toll Road, the fastest exit out of inner city traffic and toward the Silver Spurs Ranch.

His phone rang before he reached the toll road. Hade Carpenter had been located. Zach was not going to like the news.

KALI WATCHED in amazement as the ranch took on the appearance of a crime scene. The new activity put Saturday morning's investigation to shame.

This time Sheriff Ed Guerra and his team of khaki-clad crime experts were going through the stable with such intensity that she was quite certain they could have found the proverbial needle in a haystack had there been one.

And not surprisingly a news team from Houston

had shown up and endured the sheriff's consternation and orders to stay out of the way long enough to take some video of the search. They'd even done a brief interview with Kali that had made her so nervous she'd probably sounded as distressed as she felt.

Fortunately, the weather was cooperating. The forecast had said there was a fifty percent chance of thunder showers, but so far the sun had taken control of the skies. And in spite of the fact that it had been freezing just two days ago, the temperature was already in the mid fifties and still climbing.

The sheriff had ordered her to stay out of the way with only slightly less vehemence than he'd used with the reporters. She hadn't exactly cooperated with the command. Unfortunately, it was more dread than morbid curiosity that had her creeping close to try and take in everything that was going on.

It further aggravated her that Jim Bob had been welcomed into the search although he was no more a law-enforcement officer than she was. Currently he was scavenging through some old, rusted equipment that had been dumped behind a small storage building a hundred yards or more from the house.

"You'd be more comfortable in the house."

She turned to find the sheriff a few steps behind her, his shirt smeared with what looked like black grease, his hat pulled low over his forehead. His face was red from the wind and sun and his sleeves were rolled to the elbows revealing a couple of scratches he'd probably picked up during the morning's search.

"Have you found any more evidence?" she asked, ignoring his suggestion.

"Not yet, but we're going to stay at it until we're sure we haven't overlooked anything."

"Maybe you should have called the Houston CSI team. I'd guess they have a lot more manpower and they seem eager to help in the investigation."

"It's CSU in Houston—crime scene unit. And to answer your question, this is my county, and if one of my citizens is in danger, then I plan to be in charge."

"But you did let Aidan know about the skirt?"

"Not yet."

"He probably knows anyway," she said. "I called Zach Collingsworth and told him. They were together at the time."

The sheriff kicked at a pebble with the scuffed toe of his boot and shook his head. "Then I reckon he'll be showing up any minute. Not that I mind working with Aidan on this. It's just not his show. That's all."

It was even less Zach's show, but she hoped he would be out here soon. Her good intentions to avoid letting him get too close might have worked if the ranch had been as peaceful as she'd remembered it.

Instead she'd been hit with one gruesome discovery after another. Talk of murder monopolized every conversation. The aura of death cast a gray film over everything in sight. And when she closed her eyes all she saw was blood and blank, hollow eyes staring at her.

With all that to face, she simply couldn't refuse

Zach's help any more than she could stop her heart from reacting to him.

A sputtering roar drew her attention to the road in front of the house. A lone rider on a motorbike that looked sizes too big for the petite figure slowed and finally came to a stop. It wasn't until the rider removed the helmet and goggles that Kali realized the visitor was Jaime and not another cop.

She smiled and waved as she climbed from the bike. Her mass of disheveled blond hair fell over the shoulders of her sleek black leather jacket. And still she was gorgeous.

Jaime looked around and waved in the direction of Ed Guerra and a couple of his deputies who'd just rounded the corner from the back of the house. "Zach called and said you might need a rescue from the havoc going on around here."

The fact that he was worrying about her pleased her more than a little. "That was thoughtful of him, but really I'm fine. Well, perhaps *fine* isn't the word, but I'm making it."

"I've been ordered to invite you to Jack's Bluff for lunch and Zach insisted that I not take no for an answer. Besides, we didn't have much chance to talk yesterday. We need to catch up on the—what is it?— fifteen years since you were last at the ranch."

A normal conversation over lunch sounded like heaven, and surprisingly she was hungry. "It would be nice to get off the ranch for a bit and away from the talk of killers and bloody evidence."

"Great. I brought an extra helmet in case you were game to ride behind me on the bike. Zach can bring you back. He's on his way home and I'm sure he'll be there by the time we finish chatting. But he wants Jim Bob to follow us home. He's really worried about you since they found your picture in that shirt pocket."

Kali's first instinct was to refuse the ride and have Jim Bob ride with her in her Jeep. She'd always been a coward when it came to speeding down a highway with nothing between her and the road but a couple of tires and a roaring motor. But after this week, riding behind Jaime seemed downright tame.

"Let me tell the sheriff where I'm going and grab a jacket, and you're on," she said.

"While you're doing that, I'll get Jim Bob."

The sweet relief of getting away from the horror at least for a while swept though Kali, but died the second she approached the front door of the house and had to walk over the spot where she'd found Louisa Kellogg's body.

Lunch at the Collingsworths might provide a momentary diversion, but the nightmare wasn't going anywhere until the killer was arrested. Even Zach, with all the Collingsworth money and clout, couldn't change that.

ZACH'S STOMACH knotted at the news Aidan had sent via text message when he couldn't get through with a phone call. This was the last thing Kali needed to hear today. He wondered if she'd heard already. He'd find out soon enough. With luck she'd be at Jack's Bluff having lunch in an environment not crawling with cops.

It was nearly one o'clock when Zach parked his Jag in the drive at the big house. There was no sign of Kali's Jeep. Either she'd turned down Jaime's invitation for lunch or else she'd come and gone. Hardheaded as she was, she'd probably refused to leave the ranch.

But both Matt's and Bart's trucks were there. They seldom missed lunch at the big house. As Matt said, nothing worked up an appetite quicker than fresh air and ornery cows.

Zach's heels clicked on the wide slats of the porch as he crossed it and opened the front door. It was unlocked, as usual. A few miles and a world apart from the Silver Spurs Ranch where Kali guarded admittance with a shotgun and bloodied garments hid in wet leaves and lay buried in dry hay.

Odors drifted from the kitchen, chilies and spices and fried fish. He heard Bart's voice before he got there, his tone serious enough that Zach knew this wasn't the typical noon chatter.

The words were punctuated by the rhythmic tapping of his grandfather's cane against the tile floor, his signal that either he or his plate needed attention. They all looked up when Zach entered, but his eyes immediately found Kali's.

He'd expected the added stress of the day's events to be mirrored in her eyes and etched into the lines of her face. Instead she looked as if she'd just stepped from the shower, her face clean and shining and makeup-free, her auburn hair falling carelessly about her pale-green sweater.

She was spunky, that was for sure, but he wondered how long she'd be able to keep it up when all the news coming at her was bad. And now he'd have to hit her with another downer.

"Sit down. I'll get you a plate," Juanita said, her eyes lighting up at the sight of another mouth to feed. "I've got fresh cooked *pez* for your tacos."

"Fish tacos. Now there's a reason to come home for lunch."

"And here we just thought you'd escaped Collingsworth Oil and were on the run," Bart said.

"That, too," Zach agreed.

"Melvin called a few minutes ago," Jaime said. "He wants you to call him."

"Did he say why?"

"No, but he sounded irritated."

No doubt because Zach had blown off his meeting. He'd give him a call, apologize and tell him that his venture into the oil business would just have to wait a few more days. It wasn't as if they actually needed him.

Juanita returned a few minutes later and placed a heavy pottery plate holding two large corn tortillas filled with snapper, shredded green cabbage, *pico de gallo* and her secret sauce. The hunger pangs finally kicked in and Zach took a huge bite.

Talk was light at first, but had turned back to the murder by the time Zach finished his tacos. He'd just mentioned Tony Pinter's name when his grandfather tapped his cane loudly and broke into the conversation.

"Tony Pinter did it."

Zach stared at his grandfather. He was staring back and looking completely cognizant.

"What did you say?" Matt asked.

"Tony Pinter. He's your killer."

Zach swallowed. "What makes you say that?" he asked, amazed that his grandfather had even picked up on the conversation.

"He killed a man up on Lake Conroe one night. I was there."

It was the most coherent Jeremiah had sounded since before his stroke, yet Zach had trouble believing his statement was accurate. "When was this?"

"What?"

His attention span had gone south, more reason not to believe what he said. Yet Zach wasn't ready to let this go. "Tony Pinter, Grandpa. You said he killed a man."

"Who is Tony Pinter?" Kali asked.

"He was your grandfather's foreman for the past few years. I'll fill you in with the details later."

Jeremiah propped his elbows on the table. "He went crazy. Shot the guy in the parking lot. Up at Pathos Bar."

"If that happened it must have been a long time ago," Bart said. "I don't recall any murder charges against him while he was working for Gordon Cooper."

"I can see him going crazy and getting violent though," Matt said. "He drinks enough to float a bass boat and when he's drunk, he has a temper. I saw him punch out a guy's lights outside Cutter's Bar one night for spilling a drop of his beer on him."

Kali wrapped her hands around a glass of iced tea. "Why would my grandfather hire a man like that?"

"Good question, but it doesn't matter much now," Zach said.

"I need to get back to my ranch at once," Kali said. "The sheriff will want to talk to Jeremiah."

But Jeremiah had checked out of the conversation again. He was staring into space, drool forming on his bottom lip. Jaime leaned over and wiped his mouth with his napkin as he began to tap his cane against the floor.

"Do you want to go back to your room?" Bart asked, already getting up from the table to help their grandfather out of his chair.

Jeremiah brushed his hand away. "I don't need help."

Bart helped him anyway, making sure Jeremiah was steady on his feet before backing off and letting him shuffle away from the table and back to his room. Zach doubted there would be much chance of getting him to elaborate further on Tony Pinter. But if Pinter had killed a man, there would have to be a record of that.

"I have to get out of here, too," Bart said. "I want to stop at the house and see Jaclyn before I go back to work."

"In that case, I'll fix her a plate," Juanita said.

"Oh, no you don't. The reason she passed on lunch today was because she said eating your fabulous cooking twice a day was making her fat. She's probably munching on celery and carrot sticks."

"Carrots." Jaime made a gagging noise. "I'll sign her up to work with me on Mom's do-gooder riding program for underprivileged preadolescent monsters. They'll run the pounds off her."

"That sounds like an interesting program," Kali said as she and Jaime started carrying serving dishes to the kitchen. "Maybe I can help with that when my life settles down."

"Good idea," Jaime said. "You could take my place except that Mom would only find another project to keep me busy."

Zach and Matt gathered plates and eating utensils. Bart was already grabbing his black felt Stetson and scooting out the door, eager to get back to his Jaclyn. Married for only months and the guy was still so much in love he hated being away from her.

Kali stopped at Zach's elbow. "I really do need to get back to the ranch," she said. "Can you drive me, or should I get Jim Bob to take me home?"

"I'll take you, but we need to talk first."

Her brows raised. "About what?"

He didn't want to frighten her more, but he couldn't soft-pedal the danger, either. "I have the latest news on the whereabouts of Hade Carpenter and more on Tony Pinter."

"What have you heard?"

Dishes were clanging in the background and the house phone was ringing. Jaime ran to grab it, since it was most often for her. This wasn't the best place for going into his latest protection plan, especially if she protested.

He placed a hand on Kali's shoulder. "I'm going to saddle up the horses. You could use a ride, and we can find a quiet place to talk."

"Is the news that bad?"

"No, but I figure that's the only way I can get you alone."

"You're lying, but saddle up the horses. I am most definitely in need of a fast gallop and the feel of horseflesh beneath me. At least that shouldn't come with any harsh surprises."

Unfortunately, it would.

Chapter Eight

The horse Zach chose for Kali was a magnificent black quarter horse, aptly named Beauty. The spry mare was approximately fifteen hands high with two almost indiscernible white markings on her nose. Her mane was luxurious, her legs well-muscled.

"She's absolutely majestic," Kali said. She approached the animal slowly, letting Beauty get used to her odor and the sound of her voice before rubbing her sleek neck and back. "Is she yours?"

"No. Beauty was a birthday present from Langston to his wife Trish, but now that Trish is pregnant and busy with planning the cottage they're building here on the ranch, she isn't riding as much. She'll be glad to know you took her out for a good gallop."

"You're going to have a baby in the family. That's terrific."

"Why do women always gush when I mention Trish's pregnancy?"

"Don't tell me you don't like babies?"

"They're okay, as long as their diapers are dry and unsoiled and they aren't wailing."

"Even then they're adorable. I want a houseful one day. Don't you?"

"Never thought much about it."

She shriveled into herself like a dried prune. How had she ever asked such a question? No telling what he'd read into that.

Beauty looked at Kali and stamped her front hoof as if she were reminding Kali that she was to be the center of attention here. Kali delivered an apology as she scratched the mare's nose. "You are just as cute as any baby," she assured her.

The stress to her muscles seemed to fall away as she crooned to the horse and looked into her wide-set eyes. She'd always been more comfortable with horses than people. They never cared or misread you if you tripped up with your words.

It was actions that mattered with horses. Treat them right and they repaid your efforts with loyalty and a great ride. Treat them badly, and they'd let you know their feelings about that, too, but they were usually quick to forgive once you'd righted the wrong.

Zach assisted as she slid her foot into the stirrup and eased into the saddle. The reins gave her a surge of control that she hadn't felt since arriving in Texas. Anticipation skipped along her nerve endings. Even she hadn't known how much she needed this ride.

Zach climbed into his own saddle and looked back to see if she was ready to ride. He'd changed back into jeans and a light-brown sweatshirt that made his eyes look as if they were glazed in dark chocolate. Her pulse quickened and she looked away quickly. He might turn her inside out with just a glance, but she didn't have to let him know that.

"Are you ready?" Zach asked.

"Past ready, and from the way Beauty is stretching her neck, I'd say she is too."

Zach took his horse to a canter, but quickly moved to a full gallop. Kali took her cue from him, grateful for the wind in her face and the exhilarating speed. This is how she'd imagined her life would be when she'd first heard that she'd inherited the ranch. Except only in her most wanton dreams had she ever imagined Zach riding with her.

They rode past wide pastures all fenced and cross fenced, then followed a shallow creek through a cluster of hackberry, oak and towering pines. They spooked a group of deer who looked at them curiously before racing into an area where the pines grew tall and thick. By the time Zach finally slowed his steed and brought him to a stop, her heart was pounding from the exhilarating ride.

He dismounted and tied his horse to the trunk of a willowy sweet gum tree. She was already climbing off her horse when he extended a hand to help her. His touch was casual, yet a shot of heat ran the length of her arm and settled in her chest.

She handed him the reins and turned away, walking over to the bank of a narrow river that meandered through the trees. "It's beautiful out here," Kali said. "So peaceful and quiet."

"This is the spot where my buddies from town and I played pirates when I was growing up. There's probably still buried treasure beneath a couple of these trees. Mostly plastic doubloons we brought back from Galveston Mardi Gras parades."

"It must have been exciting to grow up with Jack's Bluff as your playground."

"It was, but when it's all you know, you tend to take it for granted."

She settled on a flat rock and stretched her legs in front of her. "It seems a shame even to talk about my nightmarish life in a place like this."

"The nightmare is only temporary. This will be over and done with and the killer will be in jail before you know it."

"Then you must know something I don't."

"I know that you have Ed Guerra and Aidan Jefferies both doing all they can to work through the clues and come up with the identification of the perpetrator. You can't get better than that."

A rabbit hopped into the clearing a few feet in front of Kali, wiggling its cute nose as it checked out the intruders. Apparently not liking what it saw, it turned and ducked into the underbrush, its furry tail the last thing to disappear among the vines and leaves.

Kali wished it was that easy to run away from her problems. But there was no getting away from them and no use to put off the inevitable. "Tell me about Tony Pinter."

"Not a lot to tell, except that he was your grandfather's foul-mouthed, bad-tempered foreman. Only, for some reason he and your grandfather seemed close and some people speculated that he might inherit the ranch when Gordon died."

"And you think he's a murder suspect?"

"It's a possibility."

"I can see that he might be upset with me that I inherited the ranch, but that wouldn't explain his killing Louisa Kellogg."

"No, but he's definitely got ties to the Silver Spurs. Aidan is going to track him down so that he can be questioned. Even if he's innocent, he might be able to lead them to another suspect."

"That sounds reasonable. You said there was news about Hade Carpenter as well."

"He's no longer in Cincinatti."

"Where is he?"

"Aidan's tracked him to a rented mobile home in a trailer park about thirty minutes from the Silver Spurs."

Shock and a bit of fury raced though her. "Why would he be there?"

"That's anybody's guess, but he told the manager of the apartment complex where he was living in Ohio that he'd inherited a ranch in Texas."

"I should have known he meant it when he said he wasn't giving up. But he doesn't have a legal leg to stand on. He's exhausted all his appeals."

"Maybe he thinks you'll hate ranch living and go back to Atlanta."

"More likely he thinks he can make my life so miserable, I'll be forced to cut and run. He's the type who'd go to any extreme to get what he wants."

"Even murder?" Zach asked.

"I can't believe he'd go that far. No sane person would."

"You'd think, but look at the murder rate. And Hade would have motive and opportunity."

"Now you're talking like a cop."

"Must be Aidan rubbing off on me. But it doesn't take a cop to know that you shouldn't be living out on that ranch by yourself until the killer is behind bars."

"Most of the time my ranch has been crawling with cops."

"But not always. I think you should move into the big house at Jack's Bluff. There's plenty of room. You've already hit it off with Jaime. Juanita loves having more people to cook for. The housekeeper is here three days a week so you wouldn't be putting anyone out. And my mother's always thrilled to have guests. It's the perfect solution."

"That would be just the kind of thing a scoundrel like Hade would use to revive his claim on the ranch. Besides, if there is a risk to me, I can't pull your family into it. I probably shouldn't even be here today."

"I was afraid you'd say that. That's why I have another plan."

"The plans aren't yours to make, Zach."

He reached down, took her hands, and pulled her to a standing position, stopping her protests with a brush of his lips against hers that sent her heart into meltdown.

"I'm moving in with you until this is over. Period. No arguments allowed."

She trembled as she looked into his eyes, overcome by emotions she didn't fully understand and was afraid to examine. "Why are you doing this?"

"I want to be a hero?"

"I want the truth, Zach."

"The truth isn't all that complicated. You need someone to make sure you don't become a victim. I'm available and a damn good shot."

"You have your own life. I'm not your responsibility."

"This isn't a big deal, Kali. Believe me, I'm not needed anywhere else right now and I'd much rather be with you and trying to catch a killer than sitting in a stuffy skyscraper shuffling papers around a desk."

He'd made up his mind and she doubted there was anything she could say that would change it, not that she was sure she wanted to change it. "I don't know what to say."

"No cause to say anything."

Good, because right now she was thoroughly confused and uneasy on a number of levels. But surely living under the same roof as Zach Collingsworth was safer than facing a killer.

With the latter she could lose her life. With the former, it was just her heart at stake.

"I say we ride back to the house and I'll pack a few things to take to your place. Only thing is," he said, a teasing smile playing on his lips, "I'm not that fond of sleeping bags on short sofas."

"Then you're in luck. I cleaned the guest room this morning."

"That would have been my second choice."

TOTAL CHAOS reigned at the Silver Spurs for the rest of the day. One murder had been news. The possibility that they were looking at multiple bodies buried on the ranch was lead copy. There was a steady stream of reporters and photographers and every time Kali went to the door, blinding flashbulbs went off in her face.

It was late afternoon before she looked out the door and didn't see any vehicles parked in front of her house except hers and Zach's.

"How about a walk?" Zach asked. "I could use the fresh air."

"I could go for that." She suspected the suggestion was more to get her mind off the situation, but it was still a capital idea. She followed him out the back door and along a worn path that led along a fence line.

Twigs cracked and leaves rustled beneath the heels of their boots. Two squirrels chased each other around the trunk of a skinny pine and a mockingbird called from the bare branch of an oak tree that towered over their heads.

"This is more like the Silver Spurs I remember," she said. "Except it was a lot hotter in the summer."

"It must have been that summer for sure. You were always wanting to go to our swimming hole to cool off."

"Then you actually do remember me?"

"I remember that you were crazy about me," he teased.

Her cheeks burned. She should have known not to pursue that subject. "Do you always have such erroneous fantasies about your past?" she quipped, walking faster so that he didn't notice that she'd turned a shade of crimson. She didn't understand it. She'd almost never blushed in Atlanta.

He caught up with her and put an arm around her shoulder. "Deny it all you want. You know you had a crush on me."

She brushed his arm away. "I don't remember it, but if I did, I'm well over you now."

"We could work on that."

"Dream on."

"So why didn't you ever come back to the ranch?" he asked. "That quarrel between your father and your grandfather couldn't have lasted forever."

"You obviously don't know my dad. Anyway, Dad divorced me and my mom when I was in the eighth grade and started a new life with one of the company's barely legal secretaries."

"Tough call divorcing your kid. What exactly does that mean?"

"I didn't fit into his new life, and after a few visits I

gave up. He was clearly relieved. And he had more excuses for not paying child support than Paris Hilton has party dresses. So after that it was just me and Mom."

Zach pushed back a low-hanging limb and held it while she passed. "Rotten break. Kind of hard for me to imagine having too little family."

He stopped and looked around, letting his gaze linger on a cluster of trees to the west of them. "It's getting darker. I think we should start back."

His tone was still light, but apprehension slithered up her spine all the same.

"So, did you leave a broken-hearted boyfriend in Atlanta?" Zach asked.

"Not even a slightly depressed male companion."

"Why not? Surely Atlanta guys know a nice-looking woman when they see one."

"I haven't dated much over the past few years. I spent every extra minute with my mother during her battle with cancer and after that I was working two jobs to pay her medical expenses and then I was faced with all the court and attorney fees to fight Hade for possession of the Silver Spurs. That's why money is so tight right now."

"Guess you wish now you'd given up the legal battles and stayed in Atlanta."

"No way!" The words flew to her mouth before she thought about them, but they were absolutely the truth. "Inheriting the ranch was my chance in a lifetime to raise horses and live on a ranch. I'm not going to let some murderous lunatic snatch the dream from me."

She probably sounded like a fanatic on a soapbox, especially to someone like Zach who'd likely never had a dream that didn't come true. But she meant every word. She just hadn't intended her voice to rise or her tone to grow so intense.

"What about you?" she asked, changing the focus to him. "What are your career goals?"

"Good question. When I find out, I'll let you know." He let the conversation drop and they walked side by side in an uneasy silence until the house came into view.

"I'll bring in some more wood," he said. "There's already a chill in the air, so this should be a good night for a fire."

Could this get any worse? A night by the fire with Zach Collingsworth. A night of sensual tension that would rock her soul and try her mettle. Her stomach tied itself into a knot just thinking of how hard this could get.

She was already climbing the steps to the porch when she heard the hum of a car in the distance. She groaned. Not another reporter.

But when the car stopped she saw it was Jaime and Matt. Jaime jumped from the car and held up an adorable black puppy, a bundle of hair, ears and panting tongue.

"I brought you a housewarming gift," she called.

"But not housebroken," Matt said, when they made it to the steps. "He'll be messier than Zach."

"He's a black lab," Jaime said. "My ex-boyfriend

has six to give away so I got one for you and one for Derrick and David. Theirs is a birthday present, but they're getting it early."

"So she can start playing with it sooner," Matt said. "There's always method to her madness."

Kali took the dog from Jaime and he jumped up toward her face, his tongue slapping against her chin. That was all it took. One sloppy dog kiss and for the first time since Friday night, the horror slid all the way to the back corners of her mind.

"I love him," she said.

Jaime smiled. "I knew you would. Nothing like a four-footed friend to share your bed on a cold night."

"Ouch," Zach said, but he was smiling, too and already petting the animal who'd climbed Kali's chest and was nibbling at the collar of her shirt.

She was literally surrounded by Collingsworths, and suddenly she had the sinking sensation that she'd been sucked into a world that would swallow her whole if she let it. A world of wealth and privilege where she'd never fit, no more than she'd ever fitted with Zach. If there were such a thing as royalty in Texas, he would be the handsome cowboy prince.

She was about as far from princess status as a girl could get. But how would she resist him if he made even the slightest advance? How could she spend the night this close to him without throwing herself in his arms and ending up in his bed?

All this and a cold-blooded killer who carried her picture around in his pocket.

"A BIZARRE finding at the Silver Spurs Ranch near Colts Run Cross suggests that Louisa Kellogg might not be the only victim of the man who took her life last Friday night."

He turned up the volume, mesmerized by the news and the scene flashing across his TV screen. The small-town deputies were crawling around the Silver Spurs like hungry rats, snooping into every corner of the ramshackle stable and the nearby barn.

They'd found a tattered, bloodstained skirt in a stall and they were jumping to all sorts of conclusions, or at least the young female reporter would have you believe that.

The camera moved and he caught sight of Kali Cooper standing in the background next to some curly-haired cowboy. He should have taken care of her the other night. It would have been so easy then, but she'd caught him off guard with her untimely arrival.

And even when he'd lingered in the woods and watched her enter the house, he wasn't certain that no one was following her. As it was, sirens had sounded minutes later and he'd taken the back roads out of there in the nick of time, intentionally leaving behind the shirt that would confuse them even more.

The camera moved to a close-up of Kali and he could see the lines of her soft lips and the swell of her jacket over her breasts. He imagined his hands circling her slender neck, then releasing their hold to slide down her naked body.

Best of all he imagined the scream that would

gurgle in her throat when he played his torturous games. She'd robbed him of all that with Louisa, but he'd recapture it with Kali and it would be extra-sweet. It would be his revenge.

He listened as the reporter hugged the microphone and started talking about Kali again.

"Kali Cooper says that she won't be frightened off her own ranch, and that she is confident that Louisa Kellogg's killer will be arrested soon."

Sure, Miss Kali. Good always overcomes evil. People continued to believe that myth in spite of the crime and corruption that surrounded them.

The reporter switched to a new story, and he went to the kitchen for something to soothe the pain that was striking between his temples with ever-strengthening force. The doctors made light of his complaints. But he knew what he knew. His pain was real, and murder was the only release.

Chapter Nine

Kali was riding a magnificent black horse through soft green meadows, moving swifter than the wind. Exhilaration swept through her, heightening every sense. She could taste the sweetness of the air as it rushed into her lungs, and she could feel the excitement soaring along every nerve ending.

She could ride like this forever, chasing rainbows and dreams and a thousand tomorrows. But her horse slowed and her heart began to race, a rapid drumming that filled her chest with anticipation. She knew that every step the animal took was leading her to a secret rendezvous with passion.

The horse neighed and came to an abrupt halt beneath a cluster of towering trees. Two strong arms wrapped around her waist and pulled her to the soft pine-straw carpet. And then she was in Zach's arms and his lips were pressing into hers. Desire burned inside her, hot and wanton and she kissed him over and over until her lips ached and her lungs begged for breath.

He fell to the ground and pulled her down beside him. He undressed her slowly, his fingers brushing her breasts and slipping between her thighs. She ached for him, wanted to feel his flesh next to hers, needed him so desperately she could barely breathe.

And then she glimpsed the glint of the sun off cold metal and saw the barrel of a pistol aimed at her head. Zach disappeared, taking the passion and erotic cravings with him and leaving only a cold, hard knot of fear.

The sound of a gunshot roared in her ears as the bullet split her brain like an ax.

Kali awoke with a start and stared into the darkness for long, frightening moments as the images slowly receded into the dark corners of her mind. Just a nightmare, but the passion and the fear lingered. She stretched and felt the dampness on her skin. She'd broken into a cold sweat and her pajamas stuck to her like wet paint.

The puppy sleeping at her feet wakened, too. He crawled up beside her and snuggled against her, his head burrowing in the crook of her arm.

"Just a dream, my sweet puppy," she whispered.

She held the tiny ball of wiggling life in her arms. Sweet puppy. That fit him. *Chiot doux,* if she remembered her college French correctly. "That's a good name for you—maybe Chideaux for short, which gives it a nice Cajun flair. After all Colts Run Cross isn't that far from Louisiana."

His tail wagged appreciatively, and he crawled

higher to lick her cheek. The action tangled his paws in the sheets and he whimpered in protest. She freed him from his predicament and held him close, thankful for his company as the cold fear of the killer and the hot passion from the dream mingled in her mind.

She closed her eyes and thought of Zach, her heart and body aching to cross the barriers that separated them. Two doors. A few feet.

A world of differences.

And therein lay the rub. He was here because he thought it was the right thing to do, not because of any overwhelming attraction he had for her. He'd never given her any reason to think differently.

But she knew he wouldn't hesitate to hold her, to caress her, to make love to her. Then, when this was over, he'd go back to his life as a Collingsworth heir, his duty done, his heart intact.

That didn't make him any less a hero.

If she lost her heart to him, she had no one to blame but herself.

LENORA WALKED into Langston's office at exactly ten forty-five on Tuesday morning. She'd always been prompt and organized, and when she'd taken on the job of acting CEO, the traits had become her saving grace. With the countless meetings she had to attend and the myriad projects she had to oversee, there was simply no time to waste.

"I hope I didn't mess up your morning," Langston said, "but I need to apprise you of a situation that's come up. I would have talked to you yesterday, but I was tied up most of the morning and you were out of the office in the afternoon."

"I took some time off to go to a school play that Derrick and David were in," she said, determined not to sound apologetic. She put in her share of hours and the boys were important.

Besides, Langston wasn't her boss. If anything she was his, though she never thought of it that way. He knew far more about running the business than she did. "What do you need to talk about?"

"The CIA situation."

"We have a CIA situation?"

"According to the CIA, we do, or at least Collingsworth Oil does."

She dropped to one of the leather chairs facing his desk. "This sounds serious."

"As serious as funding terrorists."

The comment shocked her and her apprehension level climbed steadily as Langston explained the allegations.

"We have to find out if there's any truth to their assertions," she said.

"I'm working on it. Melvin thinks we may be targeted by someone who'd like to see us go under."

"I'd hate to think we have those kind of enemies."

"It's a crazy world out there, and with our operations in the Middle East, we make a convenient mark."

"You said Zach was in on the meeting with the CIA agents. What was his take on the situation?"

"He agrees that we have to get to the bottom of this as quickly as possible."

Lenora thought of Jeremiah and the great leadership abilities he'd had before the stroke. If he was his old self and the CEO now instead of her, he'd be able to offer Langston some sound guidance. It wasn't the first time she'd realized her limitations. "Do you have an action plan?"

"The beginning of one. I thought I'd run it by you before I put it into operation."

Strictly protocol she was sure. He'd know the scope of the problem was way beyond her expertise. "Let's hear it."

"Melvin's offered to take on the investigation full-time if I'll relieve him of his current responsibilities."

"Won't he need help from experts with experience in uncovering espionage and illegal covert activities?"

"We talked about that. I'll authorize full approval and funding for him to hire whoever he needs. I'm making this a top priority. I'd hate to have one penny of Collingsworth funds diverted to terrorist activities."

Lenora took a deep breath and exhaled slowly, then stood and walked to the window. She gazed at the spectacular view of downtown Houston with its gleaming skyscrapers and steady stream of traffic. It constantly amazed her how well Langston fit into this world and still seemed so at home on Jack's Bluff.

Of all her sons, he was definitely the most suited to the high-stress dilemmas associated with running an international business. He was not only brilliant and level-headed, but also his value system was strong and intact.

"Your father would be incredibly proud of you, Langston. So am I."

He joined her at the window and put a hand on her shoulder. "Thanks. And for the record, I'm proud of you, too."

"Because I didn't lead the company to ruin when I took over as acting CEO?"

"That, too. But I was referring to the fact that you're one terrific mom. You always have faith in me, and that makes all I do easier."

She blinked fast, holding back the ridiculous moisture that pooled at the back of her eyes. "I say go ahead with your plan of action," she said.

"Good. I'm hoping to enlist Zach to work on the project with Melvin, that is if I can ever get him to show up at work for more than a couple of days in a row."

Lenora's motherly defense mechanism checked in. "I know he's been hesitant to commit to a career in the past, but it isn't like Zach's out goofing off this time, Langston. He's working to make certain Kali Cooper is safe. I think that's very responsible of him."

"Are you sure he's not just making a play for Kali?"

"He's been involved with lots of women, Langston. I've never known him to put himself out like this for any of them. He seems truly concerned."

"Aidan said the same thing," Langston said, "so maybe you're right and he is doing this for purely un-selfish reasons and not out of lust."

"I think we should give him the benefit of the doubt."

"Spoken like a mom."

"And if I didn't stand up for him you would," she said. "How many times have you said that when he finally got it all together, he'd be a monumental success?"

"I guess I just have trouble understanding him and Jaime. The rest of us all have discovered our forte. The oil company has always been exciting for me. Bart and Matt love ranching. Becky's calling is definitely in being a mother to Derrick and David—at least for the time being. It's only Jaime and Zach who are still finding themselves."

"Life isn't a business, Langston. You can't put it on a timetable, and I *never* compare my children."

"You're right, of course. Who am I to decide what's right for Zach? I just hope he finds his calling soon and one day ends up as much in love with the right woman as I am with Trish and Bart is with Jaclyn."

"Me, too," Lenora admitted. She wished for love for all her children.

In minutes she was on her way back to her office. She was concerned about the CIA problems, but there was no short-term solution for that. More immediate were her concerns for Zach.

Our youngest son reminds me a lot of you, Randolph. You were always so fiercely protective, a man's man in every way, the cowboy who stole my heart with that first smile. Zach has your smile, too.

And he's proving how caring and conscientious he can be when he truly feels needed.

Some people might think it strange she still talked to her husband after he'd been dead for over twenty years, but she'd given up worrying about it years ago. He was still in her heart, so why wouldn't she talk to him?

Lenora stopped at her office door, not quite ready for the next task. She closed her eyes and whispered a prayer. "Keep Zach and Kali safe. Whatever they're up against, please keep them safe."

An extra little prayer never hurt.

THE SUN was high in a cloudless sky and the temperature had climbed to seventy-two degrees. The humidity was higher. Kali had shed her jacket and was considering going back inside and changing her light pullover sweater for a cotton blouse.

She and Zach had been going through the outbuildings for the last two hours, searching through each one and trying to take an inventory of machinery and tools they had on hand. There were five buildings in all, counting the garage and the stable. So far, the exploration had been pretty much a bust.

"I hope this is the bonanza," Kali announced as she pushed through the squeaking door of the last building, a rectangular metal structure that was in much better condition than the others had been. It was also furthest from the house. They'd used Kali's Jeep to get out here and the dirt roads they'd taken seemed little more than muddy paths to her. Amazingly, they hadn't gotten stuck—yet.

Once inside the building, she set Chideaux on the floor as her eyes adjusted to the dim light. There were no windows and thus little air circulation. The building was obviously a storage facility. There were stacks of lumber in a back corner and some sort of plastic tubing lined the right wall. There was even an antique sewing machine cabinet. The machine itself was missing.

Chideaux got tangled in his own feet in his rush to keep up with Zach. She followed close behind, choking on the thick, musty air. A coughing spell left her throat even dryer than it was already.

Zach walked over to a rusted metal contraption and stooped to give it a closer look. "This thing was outdated before I was born."

"What did it do when it wasn't outdated?"

"It's a hay-baling attachment. I know your grandfather had better than this. Are you sure the equipment was supposed to stay with the ranch?"

"The will specifically stated that the money from the sale of the livestock should go to Hade, but that the farm and ranch equipment, including all tractors and vehicles, should stay with the ranch."

"I haven't seen any vehicles around here, either," Zach said. "I know Gordon had a late-model Dodge Ram truck. It should be here because it sure didn't drive itself away."

"Do you know what everyone around here drives?"

"Yep, that's how you know who you're waving to when you pass them on the road. If you don't recognize the vehicle, it's either new or the driver's a stranger."

"You wave at everyone you pass?"

"It's more of a two-finger salute, I guess. You leave your hand on the wheel and raise these two fingers." He demonstrated the action.

"In Atlanta you usually get a one-finger salute if you make another driver mad. Otherwise, they just zip right past."

"Trust me, by the time you drive that Jeep to town a couple of times, every rancher around here will know it's Gordon Cooper's beautiful granddaughter behind the wheel." He knocked a beetle from a work table that held a few screwdrivers and a vise.

Kali scanned the rest of the building. "I'd say we've reached another dead end."

Zach nodded, his face showing the irritation she felt. "Either someone stole the equipment for their own use or to sell. Frankly, I wouldn't put that past Tony Pinter. He might have figured he had it coming to him since he was left out of the will altogether."

She was starting to really dislike this Pinter guy. Her finances would never allow her to purchase new machinery. She hoped she could rent what she had to have until she could turn a profit. If not… If not, she'd be staring failure in the face—exactly what Hade Carpenter wanted.

"I think it's more likely Hade who stole the equipment," she said. "He probably headed down here as soon as the final decision came from the judge, stole the equipment and sold it. That would suit his purposes to a T. He'd have the money and I wouldn't have the equipment to run the ranch. I'd be set up to fail and when I do, he'll move in and take over."

"If that's the case, there may be a way to track down the equipment."

"How?"

"Most likely Gordon bought it in Colts Run Cross. Guy Linders runs the tractor and implement company there and he gives everyone a square deal. He'll have the serial numbers of everything Gordon bought new."

Kali brightened a bit at the prospect of recovering at least a tractor. "I think we should call Guy Linders right now." She pulled her phone from her pocket. The display said no service.

"My cell phone's not working," she said, "but the battery is fully charged."

"It's probably the metal in the building that's interfering with the signal. Try it outside."

She rescued Chideaux from beneath a piece of cardboard that he'd tunneled under and took him outside with her. He wandered away, squatted and watered a healthy weed before chasing a chameleon.

Jaime couldn't have known what a lifesaver he'd be. He was the one bright spot in all of this. Besides Zach, of course.

She didn't know she'd be getting through this

without Zach—or how she'd get through the days and nights when he left. But that was a problem for later. She checked her phone. The signal had returned, but now she was having second thoughts about calling Mr. Linders. It seemed a better idea to go and visit him in person.

Only Guy wasn't the one she really needed to see. She waited until Zach exited the building to join her in the sunshine. "I think I'll pay a visit to Hade Carpenter," she said, trying for nonchalance.

Zach put a hand on each of her shoulders and stared at her until she made eye contact. "What have you been smoking?"

"Nothing, I just think it's a good idea to talk to him in person."

"Well, you're wrong. It's a terrible idea."

She pulled away, not willing to be dissuaded that easily. "I don't see what's wrong with it. You said yourself he's living about thirty minutes from here."

"What do you think you'll gain from talking to him?"

"I might be able to tell if that was his voice on the phone Sunday night for one thing. And I'd like to ask him point-blank if he stole the equipment. I'm good at telling when someone is lying to me."

"I might agree with you if stolen property was all we were dealing with, but there's been a murder. We can't bypass the sheriff and Aidan."

"I've been thinking about that. Hade didn't murder Louisa Kellogg. If he were going to murder anyone, it would have been me, months ago, before he wasted all that money on attorney's fees and court costs."

"He's still a person of interest at this point."

"There you go, talking like a cop again."

"I'm talking good sense. You need to be listening."

"That's all I do. I listen to you and Aidan Jefferies and Sheriff Guerra. I even listen to Jim Bob. I take note and sit around waiting for some lunatic killer to call the shots."

"You haven't been sitting, and the murder investigation is in full swing. You've got the local sheriff's department and HPD on the case."

"I still don't see what it would hurt for me to talk to Hade. You can go with me, of course."

"You're damn right I'd be going with you—if you were going. Which you're not. You pull a stunt like that and you might jeopardize the investigation, not to mention put yourself in danger."

Frustration balled inside her as if she'd swallowed a softball. She needed to do something. Surely Zach could see that.

Her phone vibrated. She checked the monitor. She'd missed a call, no doubt while she was in the metal building without a signal. There was one message waiting. She punched in the number to retrieve her voice mail and waited.

"You bitch. What the hell do you mean siccing the cops on me?"

"It's Hade," she mouthed to Zach as the irate message continued to play. She listened closely, but the message was fuzzy and she still couldn't be sure if he was the caller from the other night. Her reception at the Silver Spurs left a lot to be desired.

She punched the replay key to hear the message again and to make sure she hadn't missed anything. Hade wasn't a killer. She was almost sure of that. But he was a liar and a manipulator and she'd bet money—if she had any—that he was the one who'd stolen the missing equipment.

When the message finished playing for the second time, she broke the connection. "Good news," she said, though she was sure her voice didn't convey the same message.

"What's that?"

"If we can't go to the devil, the devil will come to us."

"I hope you're not saying what I think you're saying."

"Hade's on his way to the Silver Spurs and he's livid. Apparently he had a visit from Sheriff Guerra and now he's convinced I've set him up to take the rap for Louisa Kellogg's murder."

Zach's face grew stony, though his eyes were shooting fire. "And he's coming here?"

She nodded.

"When?"

Kali pushed up her sleeve and glanced at her watch. "I'd say just about now."

Chapter Ten

Zach put in an immediate call to Ed Guerra. He got his answer service, but the sheriff called him back just as they reached the house. Fortunately, there was as of yet no sign of Hade Carpenter, though Zach was ready for him.

When he got Ed on the line he explained the message Kali'd had from Hade as well as their fruitless search for the equipment.

"I wouldn't put it past him to steal everything that was movable," Ed said. "He's riled about not getting that ranch when he thought it was a done deal. Arrogant sonofabitch, too. All wool, warp and a yard wide."

"That's pretty much what Kali said about him, though not in those words. Does Hade have an alibi for the time of Louisa Kellogg's murder?"

"Nope. Says he was alone in his rented mobile home sitting out the storm. His fingerprints are on file, though, and they weren't found at the house the night Louisa was murdered."

"Do you have his DNA?"

"Not at this point, but from the looks of things we may not have the killer's DNA, either, so there would be nothing to match it with."

"Did you get any feel about his guilt or innocence when talking to him?"

"You're just full of questions today. My gut feeling is he didn't do the deed, but he's definitely a person of interest. Is Kali frightened that he's on his way over there? If she is, I can have him intercepted."

"No. She's convinced he's not the murderer. She wants to see him so that she can confront him in person about the missing equipment."

"That might not be a bad idea as long as you're there to make sure he doesn't try anything. I don't think he's crazy enough to pull a gun when he's called and told her he was coming and is already being questioned about a murder. But that doesn't mean he won't try to intimidate her. Hell, he tried to do that with me."

"I can put a stop to anything he starts," Zach said. "I just don't want to do or say anything to interfere with the investigation."

"Not likely that you could. The very fact that you don't have the constraints on you like someone in law enforcement gives you an advantage. But don't take chances, Zach. If it comes down to self defense— well you know what to do. Protect Kali and yourself."

"That's a given."

"And thanks for the heads-up on the missing

equipment. I'll check with Guy Linders first chance I get and see if I can get some serial numbers on whatever Gordon purchased from him. If Hade unloaded it around here, I should be able to track it down. Might be a problem if he didn't buy the stuff new, unless he kept a record of the serial numbers."

"I'll look around inside and see what I can find once Hade leaves. There's a car approaching the house now."

"Is it a beige compact with a bumper that looks like it's been used for a battering ram?"

"Exactly."

"That's Hade. I can have someone there in minutes if you're worried at all?"

"I'm sure I can handle him."

"I still wish I was there to see Kali lay into him with all her heck and tarnation."

KALI WENT inside while Zach walked to the car to greet Hade. The man got out of his vehicle slowly. It had been years since Zach had run into him around Colts Run Cross, but he recognized him at once.

He'd put on weight, enough that his spare tire hung well over his belt and a second chin swelled about a flabby neck.

Hade glared at Zach. "I'm here to see Kali Cooper."

"What about?"

"I don't see that's any of your business, Zach Collingsworth."

So Hade recognized him as well. "I'm making it

my business." Zach rested his hand on the butt of the pistol at his waist, aware as he did how out of character this was for him. He'd never pulled a gun on anyone in his entire life. He didn't want to now, but he wouldn't hesitate if the situation demanded it.

Hade's eyes narrowed. "I see Kali lured you into playing her little game the same way she beguiled the judge into seeing things her way."

"Nope, I didn't need coaxing. I was an eager volunteer. And no one's playing games here. Kali is more than willing to chat with you, but there'll be no threats from you and no ranting and raving. She's been through enough over the last few days."

"And if I don't play by your rules, you're going to shoot me?"

"Let's hope it doesn't come to that. Now, do you want to talk to Kali or not?"

"It's what I came for."

"Then let's get on with it. She's inside."

Zach shadowed him up the walk and into the living area where Kali was waiting in the rocker. Hade dropped to the tweed sofa. Zach took the worn upholstered chair where he had a good view of both of them.

"Looks as if you've made yourself at home in my house," Hade said. He crossed a meaty ankle over his knee. His chinos were neatly pressed, but his black leather loafers were crusted in mud. The veins in his neck and face were extended as if the fury he was striving to control was about to bust loose.

He leaned forward and stared at Kali with a go-to-hell look plastered on his face. "What did you tell the sheriff about me?"

"I told him the truth," Kali said. "It's public record. You've fought me every step of the way for ownership of my grandfather's ranch. Now the only way you'll get it is if I don't last a year."

"The ranch should have been mine. Did you tell him that? Did you tell anyone that?"

"You only wanted it to sell. You don't love the land or the lifestyle. It was right that Grandpa Gordy left the ranch to me."

"You manipulated your grandfather and got him to change that will when he was too old to know what the hell he was doing. You're no better than a common thief, Kali. You're scum. You might have Zach and the sheriff fooled, but I know you."

"I had no contact with my grandfather. He made the decision to leave me this ranch on his own."

"He didn't even know your name. You stole the ranch and now you have the gall to try and pin a murder rap on me just to get rid of me. You're not going to get away with it. I'm not going to jail for murdering some woman I've never seen."

"If you'd stayed in Cincinnati, you wouldn't be involved in this at all, Hade."

"A man's got a right to live where he wants. I happen to like Texas."

Kali planted her feet on the floor, stopping the slow, rhythmic movement of the rocker. "What did you do with the equipment you stole from the ranch?"

"I don't know what you're talking about. I haven't set foot on this property since my mother died."

"You mean you never came back to visit the man you thought was leaving you a ranch. That's kind of cold, isn't it," Zach asked.

Hade didn't answer.

"I need that equipment back," Kali said. "If you help me locate it, I won't press charges."

"You wouldn't have to," Hade said. "The folks I'd sold it to would—if I'd stolen it. Which I didn't."

Zach studied him closely, trying to get a feel for whether or not he was the kind of psycho who could kill a young woman in cold blood. He was mean enough, and if he could beat up his pregnant wife, he could probably do most anything. But Zach wasn't convinced that he was the man they were after.

"I've said my piece," Hade said. "Stop trying to convince the police I'm behind the killing. If you keep causing trouble for me, you're gonna get back a lot more than you bargained for."

"Your threats and scare tactics don't frighten me," Kali said. "I know it was you who called me the other night pretending to be Louisa Kellogg's murderer."

Hade stood up, fisting and unfisting his scarred hands, and then reaching up to pat a pack of cigarettes inside his shirt pocket as if that would transfer the nicotine to his system. "I didn't call you before today. Maybe the killer is coming back for you. I hope he does. That would take care of all my problems."

"Get out of my house!" Kali ordered.

"I'm going. Just don't you forget what I said."

Zach ached to plant a fist in the man's face, but it wouldn't solve anything and would give Hade a reason to press battery charges against him. He didn't need that kind of complication now.

He followed Hade to the door. "I don't want to see your face around here again. And believe me, Hade Carpenter, you make any more trouble for Kali and I'm your worst nightmare."

He realized as he made the statement just how true it was. He'd taken life as it came until now, and it had always come easy. He'd never really fought for anyone or any cause. This was diffcrent. This was about murder and intimidation and a woman who was only trying to claim what was rightfully hers. He wouldn't back down from a skunk like Hade Carpenter.

Hade pulled a cigarette from the pack, stuck it in his mouth and lit it, taking a long puff and sending spirals of smoke into the air.

"And I don't like a man blowing smoke in my face." Zach yanked the cigarette from the man's mouth. "Now get out of here before I forget that I'm not supposed to shoot you."

Hade made a face like he'd just downed a shot of rotgut liquor, but he turned and walked to his truck. He didn't look back before speeding out of the drive, leaving a spray of rock and dust behind him.

Zach carefully carried the cigarette back into the house. They had their DNA.

AIDAN HAD TALKED with the crusty old rancher many times at Jack's Bluff Ranch, but it was the first time he'd been to Billy Mack's spread. He found him in his storage shed welding a piece of metal onto an old tractor.

Billy put the rod down to cool and took off his protective hood. They exchanged greetings and Billy got right to the point. "I know you didn't come all the way out here to shoot the bull with me, Aidan, so what's on your mind?"

"I have a few questions."

"And something tells me they have to do with a murder."

"Right. I'm working the Silver Spurs murder case with Ed Guerra."

"Then I guess you know that Zach Collingsworth's living with Kali so she won't be out there alone."

"Yeah. I've talked to Zach a couple of times this week," Aidan said.

"The move surprised the hell out of me," Billy Mack said. "Glad to see it, though. A good woman is just what Zach needs to settle him down. Those jet-setting socialites he dates will never make a good rancher's wife."

Aidan wasn't at all sure Zach was ready to settle down or that he had any intention of becoming an authentic rancher. But he could very well be falling for Kali Cooper.

Billy leaned his backside against the tractor. "What kind of questions have you got for me?"

"For starters, how well did you know Tony Pinter?"

Billy scratched a whiskered chin. "I was wondering when his name was going to come up in all this."

"Why is that?"

"Tony was a magnet for trouble, the kind of man who'd stake his old man to an anthill and stand around to watch the fun."

But would he abduct and kill a woman for the thrill of it? That was what Aidan needed to know. "I'm trying to locate him, but I can't find a phone listing for him and he hasn't renewed his driver's license since he lived at the Silver Spurs. Do you have any idea where he's living now?"

"He didn't mention where he was moving to me. Fact was we didn't get along too well. He accused me of cheating on a horse deal once. He blew up and tried to start a fight, but one of my wranglers broke it up. He was like that. He could be fine one moment and then blow without warning. I heard he killed a man once."

"I checked that out," Aidan said. "It was ruled self defense."

"That's not the way I heard it. All I know for certain is he's wound tighter than an eight-day clock."

"What about family? Did he ever mention kids, brothers, sisters…"

"He's got a son in the city. I think he works at the University of Houston. I'm not sure what he does there but to hear Tony tell it, you'd think he was the chancellor. More likely he cleans the johns."

Silent alarms sounded in Aidan's brain. If Tony's son worked at the University of Houston, then he might live near there as well. When Tony visited his son, it would put him in the same area where both Louisa and Sue Ann were last seen. He could have been in both their places of employment. And he most definitely knew the ranch was deserted.

"Do you know the son's name?"

"Jake, John, Jay—Gerald. I think that was it. Gerald Pinter. Tony spent holidays with him. I think Gerald might have even come out to the ranch a time or two, but I never met him."

"How big a man is Tony?"

"Over six feet, probably weighed at least 250 pounds."

Which meant he would wear an extra-large sport shirt, the same size as the shirt found on the Silver Spurs after the murder.

"Is Tony a skirt chaser?"

"We're all skirt chasers, Aidan. Some of us might never catch one, but we chase as long as we're breathing."

"Guess you're right, Billy Mack. Let me rephrase that.

"Do you know if he brought women out to the Silver Spurs?"

"Not that I know of."

"Was he a fancy dresser?"

"Hell, no. He wore tattered jeans most of the time. And flannel plaids. He was big on flannel plaids. Looked more like a farmer than a ranch foreman. Not that there was much ranching going on at the Silver Spurs toward the end. They'd sold most of the live-stock off by the time Gordon died."

"What happened to what was left?"

"The critters went to auction. I'd heard that Hade Carpenter was supposed to get the money from the sale, but I imagine Tony pocketed most of it."

"Did you ever hear him say he was going to inherit the ranch?"

"He alluded to it, kept talking about how much money you could get from selling it to a movie star looking for a tax break. I kind of thought Gordon would leave it to him as well. For some reason the two of them got along. Maybe because they were both all alone. It can get lonesome out here if you let it."

"I can imagine. Anyway, thanks for the information."

"Sorry I couldn't be more help."

"Actually you were lots of help." He'd make one quick stop at the Silver Spurs and then he was off to find Gerald Pinter. Surely a son who had his dad over for holidays would know where he was living. With luck Aidan might be questioning Tony Pinter by nightfall.

KALI PULLED the box from the bottom of the old wardrobe in the guest bedroom. She'd seen it there on the first day, but there hadn't been time to examine the contents. She probably wouldn't be doing it now except that Zach insisted they try to find records pertaining to the ranch's business affairs. They especially needed serial numbers for more expensive items.

She blew dust from the top of the carton and handed it to Zach. He carried it to the bed, stepping over Chideaux who was playing with a chew toy Zach had made for him out of a scrap of rope.

"You open it," Kali said, as they sat down on either side of the box. "I'm afraid it's full of spiders or scorpions."

"They go with the territory," he said, lifting the top gingerly and laying it behind the box.

The box was filled with memorabilia. There were notes scribbled on sheets of lined paper, greeting cards, drawings of horses and cartoon characters, an old high-school yearbook, and letters that had been opened and stuffed back inside their envelopes.

Kali picked up one of the drawings. It was a detailed pencil sketch of a horse with its front legs high in the air and its nostrils flaring. She read the name printed at the bottom. *David Cooper.* It was dated twelve years before she was born.

"That's my father," she said. "I never knew he was artistic or that he had any interest in horses. He never talked about it."

She picked up an envelope, opened it and slid the yellowed letter into her hand. "I feel like a voyeur going through Grandpa Gordy's personal souvenirs."

"Does that mean you want me to put the box back up?"

"Don't even think about it." The letter was addressed to her grandfather and it was written in beautiful penmanship. By the second paragraph, it was evident this was a love letter, though the language was stilted by today's standards. She scanned to the end to see who'd written it. Clarice Estovan.

"It's from my dad's mother," she said. "She must have written this to Grandpa before they were married. I've seen pictures of her. She was beautiful."

"Where is she now?"

"She died two years after Dad was born from complications following a routine surgical procedure. Grandpa Gordy married again when Dad was five. That wife left him when Dad was in high school. Mom said Grandpa was single for years before he married Hade's mother. Hade, of course, was grown at the time and living up north somewhere. That's about all I know of my father's side of the family."

Kali spied a square envelope edged in gold and recognized her own handwriting. She didn't remember sending him cards, but obviously she'd sent at least one. She checked the postmark. December, the winter after she'd visited him.

She opened the envelope and pulled out a gaudy, glittery Christmas card. And, oh Gads! She'd included a photo of herself, wild red hair, braces and all.

Zach leaned over for a closer look. "Let me see that."

She shoved the snapshot back into the envelope. "Not before Halloween."

He tried to take it from her and she threw herself back on the bed, holding the envelope out of reach.

"So that's the way you want it." He pushed the box out of the way and seized her waist, pulling her closer so that he could make a grab for the card.

The old mattress sagged, sending her rolling into him. She tried to duck away from him. But he was too fast for her. The next thing she knew his mouth was on hers and the room began to spin.

She couldn't think. She couldn't breathe. All she could do was kiss him back as waves of passion exploded inside her.

Chapter Eleven

Kali melted into Zach's arms and into his kiss. His hands slipped beneath her cotton sweater, his fingertips searing her bare skin.

When his lips left her mouth, it was only to trail a heated path down the curve of her neck and into the hollow above her cleavage. She slipped her arms around his neck and her fingers tangled in the thick locks of his hair as she pulled him closer.

He writhed, the hard thrust of his arousal pressing into her as he unclasped her bra so that her breasts spilled out. Her nipples arced and pebbled from the desire that seemed to be tearing her apart. Or maybe it was making her whole.

She could feel the fire inside her, a burst of liquid flame that started in her heart and traveled to every part of her as Zach lifted her shirt and put his mouth to first one breast and then the other. His tongue teased and tasted as he sucked, until she couldn't hold back the tiny moans of ecstatic pleasure.

The last few days had been so difficult, a nightmare that never went away. She needed this release. No, she needed Zach. She slid her hand between them until her fingertips brushed the intoxicating hardness of his erection through his jeans.

He made a gasping sound, as if struggling for air. "Oh, Kali. You're so...I'm..." He exhaled quickly and pulled away. "I'm sorry."

Her heart dropped to her toes. "What's wrong?"

"I shouldn't have come at you like that."

"You haven't done anything, Zach, at least not anything I didn't want. We're adults, and—"

"No." He pushed her disheveled hair back from her face, letting his fingers linger on her cheek. When she met his gaze, she could swear his eyes still burned with desire.

He rose to a sitting position and turned away from her. "I didn't move in here to take advantage of you."

She put her hand on his arm. "I'm a grown woman, Zach. I could have said no."

"But—" Zach jerked to attention and rushed to the window even before she heard the purr of an engine and the sound of a vehicle bumping and jolting along the rutted drive.

"It's Aidan," he said. He raked his hair back, then straightened his shirt and tucked it back into his jeans. "There must be some new development. I'll let him in."

All she could manage was a nod.

He left quickly and she could tell he was thankful

for the interruption that kept him from saying anything more. He was rushing to escape, but he'd been as caught up in the moment as she'd been. There was a lot about Zach she didn't understand, but she couldn't have misread his passion.

She should probably be glad they hadn't gone all the way, especially when the relationship had nowhere to go. She was on a mission and struggling to stay afloat financially until she could reach it. He was one of the most socially prominent and richest bachelors in Texas.

Stopping things before they went too far was to her advantage. So why did she feel as if she'd been slapped in the face?

She touched her fingers to her lips. They were still swollen from his wanton kisses. And she knew then, right or wrong, whatever the cost, she wanted to feel his mouth on hers again. More than that, she wanted to make love with Zach.

ZACH STRODE to the front door, his muscles tense. He felt pummeled by feelings that made no sense. You'd think he was a schoolboy making out for the first time. Not that he was the promiscuous playboy people made him out to be, but he'd been with plenty of women and with far less passion than had hit him back in that bedroom.

So why had he felt as if he were about to commit an unpardonable sin or at least cross a line that had never been crossed before?

It was the situation, he decided. Murder. Danger. Bloodstained garments and arrogant bastards like Hade Carpenter took priority over everything else. Kali might be spunky, but she was vulnerable and understandably frightened. She could easily misread their making love, might think it was a lot more than their emotions taking a fast ride on a runaway horse.

He opened the door before Aidan knocked.

"You *are* keeping a close eye on the place," Aidan said. "You must have heard me drive up."

"What kind of bodyguard would I be if I let someone slip up on me?"

"Not one I'd want working for me. Ed Guerra said he's thankful he has you working for free. It freed up the deputy he had keeping an eye on Kali and he's working one short as it is."

Zach was about to usher Aidan inside but decided to join him on the porch. "Ed didn't mention being shorthanded to me."

"Apparently one of his deputies is on his honeymoon."

"Guess that would be Okie. I heard he was tying the knot but didn't realize it was a done deal."

"Do you know everyone in the county?"

"Pretty much. There aren't that many of us. Not like it is for you in Houston. Is it okay if we talk out here?" Zach asked. "I could use the fresh air. Or is this visit about something Kali should hear as well?"

"The porch is fine."

Aidan dropped to the top step, using the support post

for a backrest. Zach sat on the other side of the step. "What brings you out here today? Another suspect?"

"A visit to Billy Mack. I'm still trying to track down Tony Pinter."

"Any luck?"

"I got the name of his son, but first things first. Ed said you had a visit from Hade Carpenter today."

"Yeah, and that is one sorry, lying, hot-headed jerk."

"Did you get any useful info out of him?"

Zach described the meeting including the assumption that while he wasn't the interrogation expert Aidan was, he was fairly certain that he had Hade figured out. The guy had more than likely stolen the farm equipment, at least what was left of it. As to murdering Louisa Kellogg, Kali had probably called that right all along. Hade was after the ranch and the money he could get out of selling it—not a jail term.

Kali joined them on the porch carrying a tray holding three cups of coffee, her new puppy following at her heels. She held the tray out toward Aidan as Chideaux checked out the new guest.

Aidan let the dog sniff his hand and then gave him a couple of belly rubs. "New member of the family, I take it."

"It was a gift from Jaime."

"You never know what she'll come up with. The dog is probably an excellent idea, though. He'll be good company."

"He already is," Kali said. "I have some sweetener

and skim milk in the kitchen if you want it. Sorry I can't offer better."

"No problem. I take it black, the stronger the better. Stale would really make me feel at home."

"Sorry. This is freshly brewed."

Aidan took a mug from the tray and breathed in the pungent odor. "I'll live a little."

Kali gave Zach his coffee, then took hers and left the metal tray balanced on the porch railing while she joined them on the steps. "Any news from Louisa Kellogg's autopsy?"

"The M.E. finished up a little over an hour ago. I don't have the printed report but there was no bruising or scratches, no internal injuries, no drugs in her system and no skin under her fingernails to indicate she'd tried to fight back."

"Does that mean she went with the killer willingly?" Kali asked.

"It suggests she could have. But then a knife at her throat or a gun at her head might have kept her from fighting back, as well."

"So there's no DNA to send to the FBI's combined DNA Index System?" Zach said.

"Not on the body, but her skirt had a lot of different colored hairs on it. Most were probably picked up in the coffee shop while she was working, but we collected and preserved them on the off chance we had a subject's DNA to compare them with."

Kali set down her coffee cup and hugged her knees. "So if the DNA from one of the hairs happens to match Hade's DNA, you'd know there was a good chance he was her killer."

"Yes, but the lack of a match wouldn't necessarily prove him innocent," Aidan said. "Not that we have a sample of Hade's DNA or enough evidence against him that a judge would give us a warrant to collect it."

"Actually, we do have his DNA." Zach explained about the cigarette.

Aidan grinned and high-fived Zach. "Like I said before, you missed your calling. You're a born cop."

"Don't tell that to Langston. He'll assign me to security detail at Collingsworth Oil and have me walking around the building at night peering into empty rooms. Not sure I could take that kind of excitement."

"What about the DNA on the skirt Jim Bob found?" Kali asked. "Did you get a DNA report back on that?"

"Not yet, but I've done all I can to pull rank and get a rush job from the lab. I'll let you know when I hear something." Aidan stretched his legs and sipped his coffee.

"So what's next?" Kali asked. "Are there more suspects, maybe wranglers who worked on the Silver Spurs over the last few years?"

"Ed's looking into that. His first priority right now is Hade and I'm still tracking down Tony Pinter. Tony shows a lot more potential."

"Billy Mack gave Aidan the name of Tony's son," Zach said, filling Kali in.

Aidan nodded. "He said Tony has a son named Gerald—at least he thinks that's his name—who works at the University of Houston in some capacity. I'll stop by there and try to touch base with him as soon as I get back to the city. I'm hoping he'll tell me where to find Tony."

"I have a friend who works in the university's Human Resources Department. I can give her a call and see if a Gerald Pinter actually works there," Zach said. "I can probably even get an address and phone number for you."

"I should know a Collingsworth would have connections. Give her a call. The name's Gerald Pinter."

Zach reached for his cell phone, got the number from information and made the call. As he expected, Alice was eager to help. She owed him big-time. After all, before he'd broken up with her he'd introduced her to the guy she later married.

He took the details she provided—including full name, address, phone number, other pertinent data and the fact that Gerald had been off work since last Friday with the flu.

"Gerald Pinter is a clerk in the admissions office," Zach announced once he'd broken the connection. "He's been in that position for two years. He's had one promotion during that time."

"And the last time he brushed his teeth was?"

"Damn, I forgot to ask."

Aidan smiled. "Good work, detective."

The compliment was appreciated, but Zach was jumping way ahead of that. "Glad you like my work because I have an offer you can't refuse."

Aidan shot him a dubious look. "What's that."

"I'm going with you to see Tony Pinter."

"Sorry, buddy. No way can I let you do that."

"I'm not exactly asking. I have the address. I can go there at will, but I'd rather tag along with you."

"What's the point?"

Zach wasn't exactly sure, but he was already in this deep, so he might as well jump in all the way.

"Call me curious," he said. "Besides, it's not as if you're going there to interrogate a suspect or make an arrest. All you're doing is trying to track down a person of interest—whom I told you about in the first place."

Aidan frowned. "What about Kali? It's not exactly safe for her to be alone on the ranch at this point."

"Don't worry about me," Kali said. "I have a gun. I'll be fine."

"I can drop her off at Jack's Bluff," Zach said, knowing he wasn't going to leave her alone. "She can visit with Jaime or go horseback riding."

"This is police business, Zach. You may think like a cop, but you're not one."

"I never claimed to be."

"I'm doing all the talking," Aidan said finally.

"Anything you say, Detective Jefferies." Zach finished his coffee and stood. " Shall we roll?"

JAIME SWUNG OPEN the front door of the house before Kali and Chideaux made it up the walk. "Zach said you were coming, but I wasn't sure when. This is perfect timing. I so need someone to go into town with me. I'm being fitted for the bridesmaid dress from hell—not that most of them aren't. I think it's a conspiracy between fashion designers and brides to keep the attendants looking like clowns."

"Who's getting married?"

"One of my sorority sisters from LSU. I broke family tradition by going to college out of state. I had to find some guys to date who didn't know my brothers. They scared off everyone I liked in high school."

"That could be a problem." Kali relaxed immediately. Jaime did have a way of breaking the ice.

"So does that mean you'll go with me and help me keep a straight face when the seamstress asks how I like the most ill-placed bow you've ever seen in your life? I swear it makes me look like I have a derriere the size of a hippo's."

"I'm not sure I should."

"If it's because my overprotective brother gets paranoid when you leave the house, we can get Jim Bob to drive us and serve as your bodyguard. Not that he can go into the dressing room, but he can wait in the car."

Zach hadn't wanted Kali to stay alone, but there was no reason she shouldn't go into town with Jaime in broad daylight, especially with Jim Bob along. It was the isolated ranch that presented the danger.

"I'd love to go with you, but I have the puppy."

"He can stay with Derrick and David. They're out in the backyard with Chideaux's brother, who unfortunately has had the name of Blackie bestowed upon him. How's that for thinking outside the box?"

"As long as he comes when called. And count me in. It's always fun to watch someone else's fashion suffering."

"The boys will squeal with glee when I tell them they get not one but two puppies to play with. Then I'll grab Jim Bob and we'll be off." She picked up the squirming puppy. "Oh, and if you're hungry, there's plenty of sandwich makings in the kitchen. Or Juanita can probably rustle up some leftovers."

"I've had lunch, but thanks."

Kali walked to the large family den to wait. You would expect a family with the wealth of the Collingsworths to exhibit at least a tinge of opulence in their home. There was none. This was a ranch house pure and simple with comfortable furniture and as welcoming and homey a feel as Kali had ever encountered. All the modern conveniences were there, but with a rugged, Western flavor.

The lamps were heavy black iron and reminiscent of those used in pioneer homes. The tables were made of hardwoods and the leather on the couch was supple and inviting. The drapes, in contrast, were light and airy, letting in lots of sunshine to play off the pale honey-colored walls and the polished plank floors.

Timeless was how Kali would describe the furnishings of the big house at Jake's Bluff.

She walked back into the foyer just as Jaime came bounding down the stairs. "Gotta haul it," she said.

"The seamstress is a fussy old bat who gets her panties in a wad if I'm a minute late—which I always am. Jim Bob is meeting us outside. I'll take Bart's truck since I have to pick up a few things for Juanita at the grocers."

"Don't you have to ask him first?"

"He won't mind. If he needs to go somewhere before I get back he'll take Matt's or his wife's car. Bart's easy. And there're always plenty of vehicles around this place."

They talked of the upcoming wedding and of Jaime's latest beau on the short trip to Colts Run Cross. And true to Jaime's word, the seamstress was stressing when they arrived two minutes late and the dress was gaudy with a large garish bow in the back. The color was nice on Jaime, though, a pale blue that accentuated her eyes.

After the fitting, they stopped for the groceries, which took twice the time it should have since Jaime had to stop and introduce Kali to a half dozen people.

"When your life settles down, I'll introduce you to some of the fun singles our age," Jaime said as Jim Bob carried the bags to the truck. "There aren't that many anymore. All my rowdy friends are getting married and having kids. Bummer."

Jim Bob climbed into the back seat of the double cab pickup as Jaime and Kali got into the front. Jaime pulled the gear into Drive and turned the key in the ignition.

"It sounds as if you're not that into your current beau," Kali said.

"I like him. I'm not planning to marry him. Next stop Laverne and Charlie's Butcher, Bouquet and Coffee Bar."

"You're kidding, right? There's not really a place like that."

"Not only does it exist, but the meat, the flowers and the coffee drinks are all fairly good, aren't they, Jim Bob?"

"I wouldn't know. Cowboys don't drink lattes."

"Then you can hang out in the butcher shop and make manly sounds around the raw meat."

"Can't. I have to keep you two out of trouble."

Kali pulled one foot into the seat with her. "Raw meat and lattes. My, that sounds appetizing."

"They're not in the same room. They're just adjoining and owned by the same couple. We also have a shop that sells high-end Western fashions and feed. Welcome to cowboy country."

At the mention of cowboys, Kali's thoughts drifted back to the morning's make-out session with Zach. Not that it had ever totally been out of her mind.

She'd been completely into the moment with no thought of regret. Zach had seemed just as hungry for her, yet he'd had the presence of mind to think about what they were doing and decide it wasn't for him. Was it really because he didn't want to take advantage of her? Or had he pulled away because he didn't want the relationship to go beyond a neighborly friendship?

For that matter, had he actually wanted to come

to her rescue, or was it expected of neighbors in Texas? There certainly seemed to be a different set of rules of engagement here than what she was used to in Atlanta.

The troublesome questions haunted her mind until Jaime pulled into a parking spot on the narrow street and announced they'd arrived.

Regardless of the name, the café was not only cozy and charming, but almost every table was taken. They ordered at the counter, then settled at a table in the front corner with a fruit-topped tart to share and tall mugs of steaming caramel latte.

Jim Bob stood in a back corner talking to a guy who was waiting for his wife to choose pastries.

Jaime stuck a fork into the tart. "I'm really glad you got to go with me today, but did Aidan really need Zach to go to town with him or was my brother just getting cabin fever?"

"I'm not sure." Unable to escape her thoughts and doubts, Kali broached the subject as nonchalantly as she could. "Does Zach share your negative bias toward settling down?"

"He's worse than me. I dated Garth for almost a year before breaking up with him just recently. And I never date but one guy at a time. It's too complicated to juggle dates. Zach's never stayed with a woman for more than a few months at a time and he plays the field, sometimes dating more than one a week."

Kali's mood deteriorated quickly. "To each his own, I guess."

"Right. I love my brother and he has lots of wonderful traits, but believe me, Kali, you don't want to fall for him." She peered at Kali over her mug. "You haven't, have you?"

"No. I hardly know him."

"Zach and I both have serious commitment issues, and not just with the opposite sex. I changed my major a half dozen times in college. I finally ended up with a degree in sociology, but the few jobs I've had in the field didn't suit me. I know I can't just float through life without goals, but I can't find anything that really excites me."

Jaime sipped her coffee and then wiped a frothy mustache from her lips. "Zach's fared no better. He loves ranch life. We both do, but he's not really into beef production. The oil business doesn't seem to fit him either."

Kali let the subject drop. Her question had been answered. There was no one special in Zach's life and that was the way he wanted it. His kisses might be thrilling. His touch might incite the kind of passion she hadn't known existed, but she'd never be more than the girl of the week.

HE SAT at a back table in the café with his cup of black coffee and a slice of lemon meringue pie he hadn't touched. He hadn't planned to drive to Colts Run Cross today, hadn't known that he would until he got behind the wheel.

The urge to at least pass by the Silver Spurs had

been overwhelming. Some people heard voices. He had tiny daggers that stabbed into his brain, releasing the venomous desires that were never fully satisfied.

He'd been at this same table when Kali Cooper had walked in, laughing and talking with her friend as if she didn't have a problem in the world. She'd never even looked his way. If she had, she probably would have missed him behind the lush flower arrangements that filled the empty table just in front of his. They were lined up for delivery to a party, he suspected, or maybe a wedding. Whatever, they served him well, affording him a clandestine glimpse of the two women.

He imagined what it would be like to run his hand up their skirts and feel the heat between their thighs. He'd never been with two women at once before, but the thought of it excited him.

He'd need lots of time with them. He wouldn't ruin it again by having to rush to the kill.

He reached into his pocket for the pain pills as the women finished their coffees and got up to leave. The cravings were running hot inside him. He couldn't wait much longer.

He didn't have to.

GERALD PINTER, twenty-eight-year-old son of Tony Pinter, supposedly recovering from the flu, had not been at home when Aidan and Zach had arrived in Aidan's unmarked police car.

They had left Zach's silver Jaguar parked at police headquarters at Aidan's suggestion. It didn't fit the serious cop image he was looking for when he had his talk with Gerald.

They had waited in Gerald's driveway for two hours. Aidan had used the time to check with one of HPD research clerks who'd been hard at it all day, digging up info on Tony Pinter. He'd discovered that Tony had owned a ranch up until seven years ago at which time he'd gone bankrupt and the ranch and livestock had been confiscated for bad debts and back taxes.

He'd been arrested once on DUI charges. He'd been high on legal painkillers at the time. The judge had ordered him to spend thirty days detoxing in a county rehab center.

Four months later he'd gone to work for Gordon Cooper. The big surprise was that Gordon was one of the major debtors who'd forced him into bankruptcy. Gordon had backed a land-development scheme for Tony that had failed to develop into the upscale subdivision he'd envisioned.

All interesting details, but they didn't indicate that he was a killer. After two hours of sitting in the cramped car, they decided to drive back to Aidan's office to while away a couple of more hours and then try to catch up with Gerald again.

"My office is at the end of the hall," Aidan said. "Prepare to be unimpressed."

"As long as you're doing what you want to do, the trappings are unimportant."

"That's what I tell myself."

Aidan opened the door. The office was only slightly larger than an SUV. His desk took up most of it, and every inch of desktop space was crowded with papers, files, notes, pens, half a mug of stale coffee and an opened bag of chips.

"I can see organization is the key to everything," Zach quipped.

"I have a unique filing system."

"I think this is the same plan I perfected in my dorm room my freshman year at UT." Zach meandered around the desk and stopped in front of a map of Houston with seven colored pins marking various locations. Two were near the University of Houston in almost the same area they'd just left.

"Does this have anything to do with the Louisa Kellogg case?"

Aidan nodded. "The pins mark the locations where seven women disappeared within the last three years."

Zach did not like the sound of that. "I thought you were looking at only one possible link."

"One is almost a perfect match. Sue Ann Griffin disappeared six months ago after leaving a pizza restaurant where she worked. The restaurant is three blocks from where Louisa Kellogg was abducted. She was never heard from again."

"What about the others?"

"Fewer similarities, but all of the women are in the twenty- to thirty-year age range. The others weren't college students and they lived in various areas of the city with no obvious geographical link to Sue Ann and Louisa."

"But none were ever heard from again?" Zach asked.

"We found the body of the first one. She was dumped in a wooded area north of town. She'd been sexually and physically brutalized. Evidence indicated she'd likely been tortured for days before she was shot twice in the head."

Apprehension knotted in Zach's stomach and he felt a powerful urge to call Kali and assure himself she was fine. He would, right after this conversation. "It seems I would remember a case like that, but I don't."

"You would have still been in Austin at UT at that time. Crimes back in Houston probably didn't draw that much attention there."

"What's the story on the non students?"

"Three were prostitutes who had a habit of changing identity and cutting out when they got tired of their pimps. One was a waitress with a drug problem. Her family thought she probably went to Mexico with an illegal she'd been hanging out with. And the fifth was a runaway. There was a good probability she ran again. There's no solid evidence to indicate their disappearances involved foul play."

"So why the pins?"

"Because none were ever seen by family or friends after leaving a café or restaurant alone, and I'm clutching at straws here."

Zach was fascinated and sickened by the facts. He

could easily see why Aidan got so caught up in his work. When he took a killer off the streets he made a real difference.

Aidan's fax machine started to hum. He walked to it and waited until the first sheet finished printing. Zach knew from the flex of his muscles as he read it that this wasn't good news.

"It's the DNA report on the blood found on the skirt Jim Bob found in the stable. It's a match for Sue Ann Griffin."

Zach felt the news's impact all the way down to the pit of his gut. At least two young, female victims had wound up at the Silver Spurs. The evidence supported the theory that a serial killer took his victims to the ranch, the same killer who was interested enough in Kali that he kept her picture in his pocket.

As far as Zach was concerned, the danger level for Kali had just multiplied exponentially.

Chapter Twelve

On the second visit, they found Gerald at home. He opened the door and stared at them questioningly. "Can I help you?"

Aidan flashed his ID. "I'm Detective Jefferies and this is Zachary Daniel," he said, using Zach's full first name and his middle name in place of his last.

Not a lie, Zach thought, just deliberately and smartly misleading. There was a chance Tony might have mentioned the Collingsworths, possibly even Zach to his son.

Aidan returned the ID to his pocket. "We're looking for Gerald Pinter."

"I'm Gerald. How can I help you?"

"Is Tony Pinter your father?"

"Yes, has he been hurt?"

"No, it's nothing like that. We're trying to locate him, and I was hoping you could help."

"Is he in some kind of trouble?"

"No." Aidan looked around then back to Gerald. "Can we come in? I hate talking in a doorway."

"Sure, detective, if you don't mind being exposed to the flu. I've been sick for several days now."

"We'll take our chances."

"It may not be worth it. I'm not sure how much help I can be. I haven't seen my father in weeks."

They stepped inside and followed Gerald through the small, cluttered living area and into the kitchen. "I was just about to warm some soup," he said, pointing to an unopened can of chicken noodle on the counter. "But sit down."

He motioned to the wooden chairs around the table. "And forgive the mess, but like I said, I've been ill."

The place showed it. Dirty dishes were piled in the sink and something that looked like dried mustard—or worse—was smeared across the counter. Empty soft-drink cans were spilling from a trash can that was sitting by the back door as if waiting to be emptied.

"We stopped by earlier," Aidan said, "but you were out."

"I had to go out for more meds and I stopped by my office at the University of Houston to get some work that I hope I'll feel like taking care of tomorrow."

Gerald finally joined them at the table. "Is this about that young woman who was killed at the Silver Spurs Friday night?"

"Then you've heard about that?"

"How could I miss it? It's on the news constantly."

"Did you know the victim?"

"No, but she attended classes at U of H. I understand she was an excellent student. The report I'm getting is that the whole school is devastated. My father worked at that ranch for years. But then I'm sure you already know that or you wouldn't be looking for him." Gerald's expression revealed his worry. "Dad's not a suspect, is he?"

"No. We're just trying to question as many people as we can who had ties to the ranch in hopes someone can give us a lead. Can you give us your father's current address?"

"I don't have it. He was renting a house in Spring, but the owner sold it and he had to vacate. The last I heard he was going to move in with a friend in Willis."

Spring and Willis, Texas, were off I-45 North, both a lot closer to the Silver Spurs than to Houston. "When was that?" Zach asked, ignoring Aidan's order that he was to leave the talking to him.

"About a month ago. He wanted to move in here. I told him no and he went into a belligerent rant. He'll call when he cools off. I know it sounds mean of me not to take him in, but he's better off having to work to support himself. Letting him lie around day after day with no responsibility only exaggerates his problems."

"What problems are those?" Aidan asked.

Gerald worried a salt shaker that sat in front of him. "You should talk to him about that."

"We will. In the meantime, it's probably better to tell us what you're talking about than have us think the worst."

"Good point, and it's not a big deal." Gerald propped his elbows on the table. "If you've talked to anyone from the Silver Spurs you likely already know that Dad likes to drink and when he's drinking he tends to become aggressive and a bit obnoxious. Anyway, once he sobers up, he's as nice a guy as you'd ever want to be around."

The fact that Tony had a temper wasn't a secret to anyone, but still Zach could see why Gerald was hesitant to say anything bad about his father. Family loyalty had been ingrained in Zach since birth.

"Lots of guys become blowhards when they drink," Aidan said, still playing it cool. "I really need to talk to him though. Just a phone number where I can reach him would be a big help."

"I'm afraid I can't help you there, either. They discontinued his cell phone service when he didn't pay his bill. Now he gets those prepaid phones and I don't have a current number for him."

"Do you know anyone who might? A friend, another relative, maybe your mom?"

"My parents are divorced."

"Sometimes divorced couples keep in touch."

"Not my mother. She's been living in Aruba for years and doesn't even keep in touch with me. The only other relative is Dad's Aunt Bertha. She has Alzheimer's and lives in a nursing home in Midland—if she's still alive. We are not a very close family."

"What about that friend in Conroe you were talking about? Do you have a name or phone number for him?"

"I'm afraid not."

"Do you have a recent snapshot of your father?"

"I do, but—" Gerald pushed his chair back from the table "—I'm afraid I've given you the wrong idea about Dad. He's rough around the edges, but he's basically just an aging good old boy. I'm positive he didn't have anything to do with Louisa Kellogg's murder. He'd never do anything like that. The person who did has to be a very sick man."

"Agreed. That's why if your father knows anything that can help us find the killer, I'm sure he'd want to cooperate."

"Most assuredly. I'll get the photo. As far as Louisa Kellogg is concerned, I can guarantee you he's completely innocent."

"They all are," Aidan mouthed as Gerald left the room. "Until proven guilty."

And before they could prove anything on Tony, they had to find him.

ZACH CAUGHT the late-afternoon traffic on the way home, making the drive take almost twice as long and giving him far too much time to think. The gritty details of the investigation fascinated him. He couldn't stop analyzing the sketchy information and exploring possible scenarios in his mind.

He'd always respected what law-enforcement officers did, but he'd never grasped the full spectrum of their duties and responsibilities. Nor had he ever realized how cutting edge and absorbing their jobs could be.

And every element of the investigation brought

him back to Kali, not that she was ever entirely out of his mind. He'd never been this caught up with a woman he was dating, never had a few kisses and touches affect him as had this afternoon's encounter in the guest room.

She wasn't gorgeous, but she was seductive and sexy in a girl-next-door kind of way. Even the spray of freckles across her nose was intriguing. And he could drown in those gorgeous caramel-colored eyes.

But her appeal was about more than looks. She was spunky and outspoken, tough as nails and soft as…well he didn't know what she was as soft as, but she'd felt damn good in his arms.

Maybe he was falling for her. That would explain why he was bound and determined to personally protect her at any cost. It would also explain why he couldn't wait to get back to Jack's Bluff to check on her and why he hadn't minded sleeping on an old, lumpy mattress the last few nights.

The idea that there was even a remote chance that this could be the real thing was downright scary. Even if it was, it didn't mean they could make a romance work. Hell, he didn't even know where he was going with his life.

But he just couldn't deal with all that now. His mind and energy had to be focused on keeping Kali safe.

LENORA PULLED a light jacket from the rack by the kitchen door and hurried to the front porch to tell Zach and Kali good night. She'd been delighted to come home and find Kali in the backyard playing with David and Derrick and the puppies.

She'd quickly changed from her CEO power suit to jeans and a sweatshirt and joined them outside. After Lenora had exhausted her energy trying to keep up with the boys, Kali had joined her on the screened-in porch for a glass of white wine and some adult conversation.

Lenora was duly impressed that Kali was not letting the problems she faced lessen her determination to make a go of raising horses on the Silver Spurs. She had her work cut out for her, but Lenora was certain she was smart and dedicated enough to pull it off.

Unfortunately, Lenora had gotten very little time to talk with her youngest son. Zach had come in just before they'd sat down to dinner and murder was not a suitable mealtime conversation, especially with David and Derrick at the table.

After dinner Bart had made some excuse for driving Zach, Matt and Kali over to his house, but she knew it was to talk more about the murder investigation. She wasn't invited, and she'd never felt so left out.

"Thank you again for dinner," Kali said, when Lenora stepped through the front door and onto the wide porch.

"You're welcome any time."

"Then you may find me here far more often than you bargained for. Juanita is a marvelous cook."

"And so is Mom," Zach added. "Wait until you make it to one of her Sunday brunches."

"I'm looking forward to it."

"Bring Chideaux back, too," Lenora said. "The boys loved having two squirming labs crawling over them while they tussled."

Kali stooped to pick up the puppy. "I'm sure the pleasure was all Chideaux's."

Matt and Billy Mack walked up from around the side of the house as Kali and Zach started toward Zach's car.

"Off so soon?" Billy Mack asked.

"I'm just a working bodyguard. I have to get back to my saggy mattress. The boss here took the good one."

Kali punched him playfully on the arm. "You can never please the help."

In spite of the teasing, Lenora sensed an undercurrent of tension which made her even more concerned about what Zach, Kali and his brothers had talked about. She descended the steps and caught up with Zach. "Be careful, son."

He wrapped an arm around her shoulders and pulled her close. "I'll be careful, Mom. You have nothing to worry about, but I guess I may as well tell you before you hear it on the news."

"Hear what?"

"The blood on the skirt found in the stables belonged to a woman who went missing about six months ago. Her name was Sue Ann Griffin and she lived and worked in the same area of Houston where Louisa Kellogg lived and worked."

Lenora felt as if someone had punched her in the stomach. "Then the fact that there's a serial killer tied to the Silver Spurs is no longer just an educated conjecture?"

"They haven't found Sue Ann's body, but I'm sure the authorities will be out there searching for it first thing in the morning."

Lenora shuddered. This was growing worse by the second. "I think you and Kali should stay at Jack's Bluff tonight, Zach."

"We're perfectly safe at the Silver Spurs. Kali has a shotgun."

"Don't joke about this, Zach. Not after what you just told me."

"What I said was that someone abducted young women in Houston and took them to a deserted ranch, Mom. The Silver Spurs is no longer deserted. I'm sure if the killer has seen a newspaper or read the news he knows that. If he does show up, I can handle it."

"You're not a cop."

"I'm a man, Mom. And a Collingsworth. We don't run from cowards who prey on defenseless women. We don't run, period. So stop worrying. Kali and I will be fine."

She nodded, but the knot in her stomach didn't dissolve.

Before Zach could walk away, Matt walked over and put an arm around both Zach's and her shoulders. "I may not be the crack shot you are, little brother, but I'm a damn sight smarter and only a phone call away. Day or night. And I'd like nothing better than to put this pervert's lights out for good."

"You'll have to get in line, but I'll holler if I need help."

Lenora waited in the yard until Zach and Kali had climbed in the Jag and driven out of sight, and Matt had driven off to his place.

Billy Mack waited in the creaking porch swing. She walked over and sat down beside him. "They should have stayed here. I don't know what Zach's trying to prove."

"Zach's not a kid anymore, Lenora. He's a grown man and he's got a mind like a steel trap. Nothing gets past him. Never has. He's not going to bite off more than he can chew."

"Those are just clichés that mean nothing. Some men at twenty-six might be mature enough to handle this, but Zach isn't. He's…"

Billy slipped his arm along the back of the swing and patted her on the shoulder. "He's your baby. He always will be. But he's stepped into the role of a man and he's taken on responsibility just as you've been saying you've wanted him to do."

"But not like this. Not when it means he may have to face a killer. He's not ready for this."

"Did you ever think that maybe he just needed a reason to become a man?"

"You mean Kali. That's the other thing that worries me. They seem so attached, almost as if they're a couple."

"Would that be so bad?" Billy asked.

"They've just met. They barely know each other."

"How long did it take you to realize you were in love with Randolph?"

"About ten seconds, but times were different then. I can't bear another hasty marriage that winds up in divorce court. It kills me to see Becky pulling so far away from Nick. She doesn't even want to invite him to the boys' birthday party."

"Even that's her decision. You can't live their lives for them, Lenora. When the birds are ready to stretch their wings, you have to let them fly off on their own."

"And what do I do then, Billy Mack? What in the world will I do then?"

He stood to leave. "You're a very smart and damned attractive lady, Lenora. You'll think of something." With that he gave a wave and walked away.

Lenora waved back, thankful he couldn't see the tears that burned in her eyes.

"IT'S HARD for me to believe my grandfather could have had a psycho working for him for years and not realized it," Kali said as she jumped back in the car after closing the gate at the Silver Spurs.

"That's all just supposition at this point. There's no concrete evidence that Tony killed anyone."

"You said Aidan is going to call for an APB on him."

"He is, but Tony is still just a person of interest."

"I for one hope he *is* guilty and that he'll confess

to everything. I know it's only been days, but it seems like this nightmare has gone on forever."

"Did you see that?"

Zach's tone and the sudden change of topic put her on edge. She stretched her neck to see what he was talking about. "I can't see anything in the dark."

"I only caught a glimpse through the trees, but I'd swear it looked like flames. It's late in the year and too wet for a forest fire." He upped their speed until it felt as if they were being hurled from one pothole to another.

She kept looking, but didn't see the bright glow of the blaze until they rounded the next curve. The fire was still mostly hidden by the thick pines that grew along the road, but a thin trail of smoke curled above the branches, confirming his suspicions.

She turned to Zach. His face was contorted into deep lines and drawn lips.

"The fire's on my land, isn't it?"

"It looks like it could be."

It was minutes more before she knew the worst. By the time Zach rounded the last curve, fire was shooting through the roof of the stable and embers were dancing like fireflies in the wind.

She grabbed Chideaux and jumped from the car the second Zach stopped. "We have to put it out before the blaze spreads to the house," she cried.

"I'll get on it. You use my phone to call Jack's Bluff. The number's programmed in. Tell them to get over here on the double. And call 911 for the

Volunteer Fire Department. We'll need all the help we can get."

And even that might not be enough. Tears burned the back of her eyelids as she made the calls. It was more than the stable that was going up in smoke.

It was her dreams.

Chapter Thirteen

By the time Zach reached the stable, the fire was a roaring inferno. The wood cracked and sizzled, spitting flames high into the air. A support beam gave way and half of the side wall collapsed, taking a huge chunk of the roof with it. Smoke poured from the burning wood, scorching his eyes and clogging his throat.

There was running water at the stable with spigots on the outside and one garden hose, but even if he could get to it, the result would be like spitting into a hurricane. Other than that the nearest water supply was a drainage ditch holding rain water and that was a good fifty yards from the blaze.

He backed off. Losing the stable was the least of his worries right now. If the fire went unchecked it could spread to the fences and house.

He heard Kali calling to him, but the crackle and crashing of another falling beam drowned out her words. She ran up beside him and grabbed his arm, yelling to be heard above the fire's crackling roar.

"I talked to Matt. He and Bart are on the way. So are the volunteer firefighters."

"Good work. Where's Chideaux?"

"I put him in the house." She looked up at the fire. "We have to do something. We can't just watch it burn."

He put an arm around her shoulders. "It's gone, Kali. The stable's past saving."

"I have to get to the hose."

She yanked off her jacket and rushed toward the scorching heat. A torchlike sliver of wood shot from the blaze and fell into her hair.

Panicked, Zach ran to knock it off her, and then dragged her away from the fire's fury. "Please, Kali, just go back to the house and wait for Matt and Bart. This isn't worth risking your life."

"I can't lose my stable. I can't." Sobs tore at her voice.

He held her close. "We don't have anything to fight it with but our hands. If your grandfather ever owned any firefighting equipment it's been sold or stolen."

"We have buckets and there's water at the house."

"You'd be losing ground hauling it."

A half dozen grassfires had popped up while they were talking. He knew it was a losing battle, but he tore off his jacket and started beating at the new fires, trying to snuff them out before they grew out of control.

Kali worked alongside him, though the smoke and heat from the fire were almost unbearable.

Finally he heard Matt's voice and turned to see his brother racing toward them. Bart was in one of Jack's

Bluff's heavy-duty work trucks, backing it up to the drainage ditch. "We brought a pump," Matt said, "and some of that outdated irrigation hose Jeremiah refused to trash. We could use your help setting it up."

Zach pulled Kali to her feet and into his arms. "We can get it from here, but I can't help them unless I know you're safe. You have to move away from the fire."

"Hade did this," she said. "He said he'd ruin me and he did."

"The stable is just wood and nails, Kali. It can be rebuilt. Now go back to the house."

"What's the use? He won't give up until he wins."

Zach would be damned if he'd ever let that happen.

A gust of wind came from the north, sending a shower of glowing embers and smoke their way. Finally Kali retreated and he ran off to help Matt and Bart.

In minutes the three brothers had snaked the black hose all around the stables and the pump was delivering a spray of water onto the parched grass. It would do nothing to slow the destruction of the stable, but it would be a boon in keeping the fire from spreading until the fire department's tanker truck arrived to extinguish the blaze.

The firefighters arrived minutes later with the county's two new tanker trucks. Together they had the capability of delivering ten thousand gallons of water to the site. The firemen sprang into action with practiced precision, not slowing down until the water was depleted and all that was left of the stable was hot glowing ashes.

Zach backed away and grabbed his first good breath. He caught a glimpse of Ed Guerra standing near the house talking to Matt. Great! Just the man he wanted to see.

The person he didn't see was Kali. Apprehension skittered along his nerve endings until he spotted her standing in the midst of the firemen pouring glasses of ice water from an oversized tin pitcher.

She looked incredibly fragile among the group of burly, masculine men. Yet she'd fought alongside him, and her face and clothes were covered in thick black soot. He ached to take her in his arms and carry her off to someplace far away where the problems of the Silver Spurs couldn't touch her. Bermuda or the Caribbean. Maybe even to Venice.

Bart walked up and clapped him on the back. "You look like you're in shock."

"No, I was just thinking what a great team the Collingsworth brothers make."

"Yeah, buddy. And we were missing one tonight. Think how good we would have been if Langston had been out there with us. Sheriff Guerra was looking for you. Have you talked to him yet?"

"No, but I plan to."

"He wants to see Kali, too."

"Guess I should rescue her from the thirsty firemen and see what he wants. I hope he's thinking the fire was deliberately set by a two-legged snake in the grass because that's my take on it."

"I agree," Bart said. "If you need a posse to go

snake-hunting with you, I'm ready, willing and eager. Kali's way too nice a woman to get saddled with this kind of torment."

"Yes, she is. And—off the record—I just may need that posse."

He bypassed Kali and went straight to Guerra. It was time for action.

Guerra looked up when he approached. "Arson," he said, as if reading Zach's mind.

"Glad we agree," Zach said. "Now what are you going to do about it?"

"I've already made an arrest. We didn't catch Hade Carpenter red-handed, but dang near it."

Zach was not sure he heard that right. "Did you say you arrested Carpenter?"

"Yep. I'd told Chester Maxwell to keep a lookout for trouble out this way until we apprehended Louisa Kellogg's killer. He was driving down that blacktop near the back gate to the Silver Spurs when he spotted the blaze. He was going to check it out when he saw this car come speeding out the gate hell bent for leather. Naturally he took chase."

"Naturally," Matt said. "I take it Carpenter was the driver."

"Not only that, but he had one of those propane torch lighters and four empty kerosene cans in the trunk of his car. He hasn't admitted anything, but we got him dead to rights, at least on the arson charges."

"So he not only started the fire, but hung around to watch it burn. Otherwise he'd have been out of here before your deputy saw the blaze," Zach said, thinking aloud.

"I'm thinking he stayed until you and Kali showed up to report the fire," Guerra said. "Maxwell spotted the car shortly after I got the report of the 911 call. I think he's our man all the way, Zach. I really do. What's the chance we'd have a serial killer and an arsonist plaguing the Silver Spurs at the same time and the perp *not* be the same guy?"

Matt delivered a congratulatory clap on the back to the sheriff. "The good news is you've got a guilty man behind bars tonight."

"Who's behind bars?" Kali asked, picking the opportune moment to join them.

Zach only half listened as the sheriff retold the story. He was bone-tired and maybe that was affecting his judgment, but while he had no trouble believing Hade set the fire he couldn't see any motive for him to have killed Sue Ann. But then he didn't see any motive for anyone else to have killed her, either.

"I hope they hang him high," Matt said.

Ed kicked back on his heels. "Unfortunately, they don't practice that much in Texas anymore."

"If they did," Kali said, "I'd love to be the one to tighten the noose."

Finally Zach managed a smile. Kali Cooper might not be as naively vulnerable as he'd thought.

KALI DRAGGED herself to the bathroom. Every muscle ached and her lungs had inhaled so much smoke that it hurt to breathe. She glanced in the mirror over the old sink. Black smudges still clung to her skin and her eyes were red-rimmed and swollen from the heat, fumes and smoke. She had never been so disgustingly dirty or so odorous in her life.

Reaching into the shower, she turned on the water and adjusted the temperature so that it would be as hot as she could stand it. Finally she started peeling away her jeans and the knit pullover that would go straight to the trash.

What a night, she thought as she kicked off her shoes and stepped beneath the spray. Her stable was gone. To someone else the loss of the nearly dilapidated structure probably wouldn't be a big deal, especially in light of the fact that there was a Silver Spurs serial killer. But lumber and manpower to build another one would not come cheap and her finances were already shaky.

She'd hoped to use her cash for horses and necessary living expenses until money started coming in. She'd just have to suck it up and eats lots of beans. She truly hated beans.

The water sluiced over her, rinsing away the dirt, and releasing some of the tension from her muscles. The fatigue eased and her mood lifted. The stables were gone, but Hade Carpenter was in jail. She hoped he stayed there for a long, long time. If he was guilty of murder, she hoped he stayed forever.

She squirted a double helping of shampoo into her hair and scrubbed the fragrant lotion into mounds of frothy suds. She left her hair piled on top of her head while she soaped her face and massaged it until even the worst of the soot had surely come off. She closed her eyes tightly as she rinsed.

She couldn't see a thing, but she heard Zach's voice coming from somewhere nearby and her heart skipped a couple of erratic beats. She'd never see him in the same way after tonight. Before, he'd been the preadolescent crush and then the gorgeous cowboy who looked so good in his jeans and Stetson that he took her breath away. Tonight he'd been pure hero.

She turned as the door to the bathroom opened and she caught a blurry glimpse of Zach through the plastic shower curtain. He was utterly naked.

Warmth rushed her system, titillating every nerve and sending heated shivers dancing up her spine. Instinctively, her hand slid to her most private area, though she wasn't sure if the movement was from modesty or the stirrings that were centered there.

"I'll be out in a minute or two and you can have your turn."

"No reason to hurry when we can share."

Her knees went weak and she had to lean against the wall to keep her balance as he parted the curtain and stepped inside. His strong arms circled her, pulling her close.

"I'm all soapy."

But he held on anyway, trailing kisses along her neck as his fingers tangled in her hair. The water poured over them sending the shampoo and soap cascading down their bodies, leaving only a hot slick film between them.

"I'll wash you first," he said "since you started without me."

"I didn't know there was going to be a party." If she had, she'd have passed out from the anticipation. She still might. Was she crazy to have these feelings in light of all that was going on? Or was it the danger that made her need for passion so strong?

Zach soaped her all over, using his palms and fingers. His hands slid across her breasts and down her abdomen, his fingers dipping lower each time. His kisses were feathery, light brushes of his lips across her mouth and neck and nipples.

"I should get your back," he whispered. "Then it's your turn."

He moved behind her slowly, but his hands hugged her breasts before he trailed his fingers down to her thighs and then around to her buttocks. His touch was excruciatingly erotic and when he slid his hands between her thighs, she felt the need flow hot inside her.

He turned to face her and pulled her back in his arms. "Wash me. But you'll have to start with my back or we'll never get there."

She marveled at the change in him as she lathered his broad shoulders and firm buttocks with soap. Mere days ago he'd pulled away when she'd been so hungry for him she'd thought she'd explode.

She rested her cheek against his wet back, afraid

to ask, but more afraid not to know. "Why, Zach? Why do you want me now when you didn't before? Is it me or is it the sense of danger?"

"I wanted you before, Kali. I just didn't want to make mistakes. I didn't want to hurt you."

"And now?"

"Now I want you so badly I can't reason or think at all. I don't know if the danger has anything to do with it. All I know is I need you, Kali. I need you so much it hurts."

Her breath caught in her throat and she wondered how she'd endure another minute without having him inside her. Somehow she managed to reach the shampoo and pour it into his hair. She scrubbed quickly, her fingers massaging his scalp while her breasts and stomach pressed against his slick back.

When he turned to rinse the soap away, she circled him and fitted herself into his arms. His kiss was pure intoxication.

She pulled away and tried to soap him down as he had her, but he took her hands in his and pulled them to his erection and then down to her own white-hot core.

"Tell me you want me, Kali. Tell me this is right for you."

"Nothing's ever felt more right in my life."

He held her close. She could feel his heart beating against her chest and his breath on her skin as he slid the long, hard length of him inside her. She gasped for breath and tried to embrace every second so that she'd have the memories stored in her mind forever.

But once he thrust inside her, the passion took hold and she became lost in the ecstasy. There was no sense of time or place. There was only Zach and the earth-shaking thrill of riding with him to an orgasm so intense she felt it all the way to her toes.

When it was over, he leaned against the back of the shower as if he were too weak to stand on his own power.

She buried her face in his chest. "Who'd have thought we had that in us after the fire?"

"Don't tell me you're satisfied."

"Aren't you?"

"Only until I get you to the bedroom and can start all over again."

ED GUERRA'S special crime unit had spent all day on Thursday searching the Silver Spurs for bodily remains. They'd found what they were looking for just before dark—shallow graves, just feet away from where the stable had stood, filled with the bodies of three women in various stages of decay. One they were almost certain was Sue Ann Griffin, though decay had rendered the body past the positive-identifiable stage.

The find had left Kali physically ill and terrified. Zach had held her together with his easy ways, his strength and his gentle touch. Making love with him had been perfect, but so was every look and every touch.

She no longer fought her fierce attraction to him.

If her heart got broken, so be it. Right now she didn't think she could make it without him in her life.

Kali put the breakfast dishes away and went to find Chideaux. He was curled up next to Zach's feet. When she approached, he wagged his tail a few times and came over to nibble her shoestring.

"Desert me when a pretty woman shows up, will you? And they call you man's best friend."

"He knows who makes the gravy in this house." She peered over Zach's shoulder to see what he was writing. His notes were sprinkled liberally with the name of Tony Pinter.

She knew that Zach was immersed to his eyeballs in the case, and thoroughly convinced that as despicable as Hade was, he had not killed the two women. As yet, he wasn't convinced that Tony was guilty, either, but he was leaning in that direction.

"I don't suppose Tony's been located yet." If anyone beside the cops knew, it would be Zach. He checked in with the sheriff and Aidan Jefferies so often they were likely considering arresting him on nuisance charges.

"No. You'd think if he were innocent, he'd turn himself in."

"He may not know the police are looking for him."

"If he's anywhere near Houston, he knows it. His name and the fact that he's being sought as a person of interest were mentioned on every TV newscast yesterday. Even if he missed the broadcasts, someone would have told him."

Kali was no longer convinced that finding Tony was all that important. Faced with conclusive evidence against him, Hade had confessed to setting fire to her stable. Now the sheriff had a lead indicating that Hade had contacted several midwest auction companies about selling farm equipment.

Knowing all that had changed her mind about Hade's connection to the serial murders. He wouldn't need motive to kill. He was evil through and through.

"I'm taking Chideaux for a walk," she said. "Do you want to join us?"

"I can't. I'm expecting some phone calls."

"You can talk and walk."

"Not this time."

"Don't tell me you left messages for Aidan and Ed again."

"No, this deals with a personal matter."

And obviously private—a fact which didn't trouble her at all. She kept telling herself that as she gathered Chideaux in her arms and carried him out the door.

ZACH LISTENED until he heard the front door close behind Kali. He wasn't waiting for a call, but he had several to make, none of which he could chance having Kali overhear. Without secrets, there could be no surprises.

He was about to punch in Langston's number when his phone rang. "Zach Collingsworth."

"Why did you drag my son into this?"

"Who is this?"

"Tony Pinter. And don't waste your time thinking up lies. I know it was you. My son Internet-searched *Zachary Daniel* in Houston and Zachary Daniel Collingsworth was one of the entries that popped up—along with your picture."

The Internet was a marvelous invention. "You need to contact Sheriff Guerra, Tony. It's urgent that he talk to you."

"You mean arrest me on murder charges, don't you?"

"You're a person of interest—not a suspect. If you're innocent, you have nothing to worry about."

"That's only true if a man has the money to hire a slick lawyer. I don't. What did you tell that Houston detective about me?"

"All I told him was that you used to be a foreman at the Silver Spurs. He's contacting everyone with former ties to the ranch."

"You had no business dragging my son into this, Zach. You and your brothers think you don't have to answer to anyone, but you're wrong this time. I'm not taking the rap for a crime I didn't do."

"No one wants you to. Just give the sheriff a call."

"When hell freezes over. But leave my son out of this. He's got nothing to do with Silver Spurs, and now he doesn't want anything to do with me."

"Listen, Tony, if you won't talk to the sheriff, talk to me. I'll do what I can to—"

Tony wasn't listening. The call had ended.

Frustration balled inside Zach. He'd had Tony on

the phone and had learned nothing. He might have just let a serial killer who'd murdered several young women in cold blood get away. A killer who carried Kali's picture in his pocket.

Zach had a sudden overwhelming urge to go walking with Kali. His phone calls would have to wait.

ON SATURDAY morning, Kali woke up to find herself alone in bed. As if that weren't bad enough, there were boisterous male voices and loud sounds she couldn't identify coming from somewhere outside her window. She fumbled for her watch she'd left on the bedside table. Seven o'clock, barely daylight.

Racing to the closet in the altogether, she pulled out the scruffy yellow robe for the first time since Zach had moved in. She shoved her arms through it, and rushed to the back door to see what was going on.

Two flatbed trucks piled high with lumber were parked in a shady spot just beyond where the old stables had stood. The foundation was all that remained since several wranglers from Jack's Bluff had come over yesterday afternoon and cleared all the debris from the site.

Several burly men in jeans and work shirts were starting to unload the wood. This had to be a mistake. She hadn't ordered any lumber. Clasping the robe closed, she took the steps two at a time in her bare feet. She had to stop the workers before they unloaded those trucks.

"Morning, Kali."

Outside, she stopped in her tracks as Langston and Bart passed her carrying an extension ladder. She shrank into the robe, embarrassed for anyone to see her like this. That's when she spotted Matt and Zach stooped over and examining a pipe in the old foundation.

"Hey, there. Nice day for barn-raising."

Kali smiled at the total stranger. Before she could ask what he was talking about, Chideaux ran up and sank his teeth into the hem of the robe, yanking it open just enough to offer a peek of her right nipple.

Drowning in embarrassment, she slunk back to the house as a half dozen more men walked past with big grins on their faces and leather tool belts cinched about their waists.

A barn-raising. He had to be kidding. People didn't do things like that anymore, did they? But why else would her yard be full of men carrying ladders, hammers and building studs?

This had Zach written all over it. It was his attempt to spit in the face of the serial killer and show him that life was going on as normal at the Silver Spurs. It was a great statement—only she didn't have money for the lumber or materials.

Zach wouldn't have taken the bargain route either. He was a Collingsworth. They didn't have to search for discounts. But she couldn't let him pay for this. It would knock the equality right out of the relationship and make her feel like another of his possessions, like the Jag or the expensive watch he wore.

She hurried back to the house to shower and dress. But first she needed coffee. She picked up the pot. It was still warm, but empty. The doorbell rang as she emptied and refilled the filter. It was tempting to ignore it and let the men follow the racket to the building site. But half the town had already seen her looking like a hung-over hussy. What difference would a few more make?

Holding the robe in place with both hands, she opened the door a crack. This time the company wasn't strangers but the entire female Collingsworth clan. At least she assumed they were all Collingsworths. She'd never met the beautiful curly-haired brunette or the petite, stunning blonde.

"I told Zach he should warn you," Jaime said, pushing her way past Kali and into the house. "He insisted this be a surprise."

"It's fine," Kali said.

"Then where do you want us to put the food?"

"Food?" She opened the door wider so all the women could get through it with their pots and casseroles.

"Just breakfast and snack items," Becky said. "We'll bring the dinner over later."

"Hi, I'm Trish. Langston's wife," the brunette said. "And this is Bart's wife, Jaclyn. I think we're the only part of the tribe you haven't met. Well, except for my daughter, Gina. I didn't want her here, I mean with the bodies and all."

"I understand. I'm glad to meet you, and let me

see if I can find a place for you to unload. My kitchen's sort of small."

"We just need a place to set up," Jaclyn said. "Bart's having tables assembled outside, but they're not ready yet. We'll serve out there."

"We've imposed on you," Lenora said. "I should have called before we came barging in. To be honest, I didn't think this was the time for a gathering, but Zach insisted. I think it's his way of making something good take precedence over the evil."

"I think you're right," Kali agreed. "Maybe normalcy is what we all need. I just wish I'd known so I could have been dressed and had things a bit more organized. I'll make us some coffee."

"I'll take care of it," Jaime said. "You need to change into something a bit more fashionable than that tatty throw rug you're wearing now."

Leave it to Jaime to break the ice. How could anyone not love her?

"Ignore my sister," Becky said. "She hangs out in one that would make that one look chic."

"Not when there are sexy cowboys crawling all over the place."

"I do need a shower," Kali said. "Make yourselves at home and I'll be back in a jiffy."

"Do you have some salt I can use?" Jaclyn asked. "I'm a lousy cook, but salt covers a multitude of sins."

"So do chipotle peppers," Trish said. "If a dish flops, I chop one and stir it in. Langston never fails to rave."

Kali smiled as she headed to the bathroom. She should have known Zach would have a marvelous family. One of the wealthiest families in Texas and the men and the women were as down to earth as a hamburger and fries. She wondered if they would be so friendly if they knew she was sleeping with Zach in the midst of this frightening murder investigation.

Not that it mattered. If Hade Carpenter was the killer—and she was almost sure that he was—he was already in jail. The danger should all be over soon.

ZACH GRABBED a beer from the cooler and stood back to admire their accomplishments. It wasn't even noon and the framing was all but finished. It was amazing what a group of guys working together could get done. He'd fretted about whether or not the timing was right for this. But he was sick and tired of a maniacal killer running their lives.

This was the kind of break Kali needed. He did, too, for that matter. Even working up a sweat had felt good. The stress had obviously gotten to him more than he realized.

Bart walked by with two tall glasses of ice water. "Slackers eat last."

"I'm supervising, not slacking off."

"Now why can't I get me a job like that?"

Zach finished his beer and was about to pick up his hammer when he felt a tap on his shoulder.

"Can I talk to you a minute?"

"Aidan, I didn't expect to see you out here."

"Something's come up that I need to fill you in on. I'd rather not talk about it with everyone around."

"Some of the women are inside. We can go out to my car."

"That works."

Zach walked at a swift pace, anxious to hear what Aidan had to say. He stopped at the first pickup truck he came to. "Is this private enough?"

"Yeah." Aidan leaned against the hood. "We had a leak in the department. I didn't want you to hear the information second-hand."

"What leaked?"

"We got the report back from CODIS. One of the hairs on Louisa Kellogg's skirt was a match for Tony's DNA."

"When did you find that out?"

"Two days ago."

Anger churned in Zach's stomach. "So even when I called you and said I'd talked to Tony, you didn't bother to give me the facts?"

"We decided to withhold it from the public in hopes that Tony would turn himself in."

"The public. Is that how you see me, Aidan? Did you really think you couldn't trust me to keep confidential information under my hat? You never even mentioned that the FBI had Tony's DNA."

"I didn't have a choice in this, Zach. The DNA was collected when he was arrested for killing that man up on Lake Conroe—the one where he got off on self defense. All of the information on Tony Pinter is privileged until it's officially released."

"You're the lead investigator. You had a choice. Did you tell Ed Guerra there was a DNA match?"

"I'm on my way to do that now."

"A little after the fact, isn't it?"

"We felt that the fewer people who knew, the less likely a leak would make it to the media before we could take Tony into custody. But we'd already decided to tell Ed today."

"So why tell me in private if the media already has it?"

"I just wanted a chance to explain why I couldn't tell you sooner."

Zach only nodded. If he said anything now, it would likely be too much. He wasn't a cop. He was just a cowboy who happened to be willing to put his life on the line to keep Kali safe.

"Is there anything else I should know, anything that's not *privileged?*"

"That covers it. And don't take this the wrong way, Zach. It's policy."

"Then I guess that concludes our conversation." Zach walked away without looking back, his mind already grappling with the new information.

His cell phone vibrated. He reached in his pocket and took the call.

"Zach, this is Tony again. You said you could help. Now I'll see if you're as good as your word."

Chapter Fourteen

Kali rummaged through the bags of picnic items Bart had stacked on the back porch. The butcher paper to top the folding tables had to be in there somewhere.

"I'm glad I found you," Jaime said.

"Please don't tell me someone else is bringing food by. We have enough to feed half the county now."

"It's not food. Did you hear about Tony Pinter?"

"No, has he been arrested?"

"Not yet, but you can bet he will be soon. They found his DNA on Louisa Kellogg's body. Well, actually they found a couple of his hairs on her skirt, but hello? No way did she hang out willingly with that lunatic. It freaks me out, though. That means we had a serial killer living right here in Colts Run Cross."

"Then it was Tony, not Hade, who killed Louisa and the others?"

"They have his DNA. That pretty much seals the deal. I thought you'd be relieved to know this whole mess might be over soon."

It was almost too good to believe. She'd be free to start acquiring horses and move on with her life. She and Zach could…

Could what? Move in together? Go back to being neighbors? She pushed the mental questions to the back of her mind. She should at least give herself some time to enjoy the good news.

"Could you take this roll of paper to Jim Bob? I want to find Zach."

"He just left, didn't he?"

"Left to go where?"

"I don't know. I was looking for him to make sure he'd heard about Tony and Becky said she'd just seen him drive off by himself. So I came to find you instead. He was probably just going to pick up some tool they'd forgotten to bring."

"Are you sure about Tony?"

"Positive. I overheard Langston telling Matt that he'd heard it from Aidan. But it's not a secret. Langston said it's been leaked to the press."

"Thanks," Kali called, already pushing past Jaime and rushing toward the front door. She scanned the area where Zach's car had been parked. The spot was empty.

She called his cell phone number. He didn't answer, and he always had it with him, especially now.

He'd gone back to Jack's Bluff for a tool they needed. He'd had to make a run into town for more supplies. She tried to spin the situation in a positive light, but trepidation poisoned the attempt. This had to do with Tony Pinter, and nothing about Zach rushing off alone could be good.

He'd taken this case personally, committed himself to making sure she was safe almost since the first day he'd walked through her door. She wouldn't put anything past him, not even going out to find Tony on his own, especially since Tony had called him yesterday.

She spotted Aidan first, standing at the side of the house talking to Becky. Impulsively she hurried over and grabbed his arm. "I need to talk to you. It's urgent."

"Sure. Excuse me a minute, Becky."

"I think Zach's gone looking for Tony," she said. "You need to go find him."

"Zach was just here a minute ago."

"Did you tell him about Tony's DNA?"

"Yeah. He was upset I hadn't told him earlier, but he'll understand when he—" Aidan's sentence dissolved into a string of curses. "Are you sure he's gone?"

"Yes. He's gone to find Tony. I know he has. Otherwise he would have told me where he was going. And he'd answer his phone."

"Damn it. Zach wouldn't have taken off so fast unless he knows where to find Tony. That was probably him who called while I was walking away. And Zach is playing right into the lunatic's hands. Okay, Kali, hang tight. I'll take care of this."

He raced to the parking lot. She raced after him and threw herself into the passenger side of his car. "I'm going with you, and don't argue. There's no time. If we don't hurry we'll never catch him before he reaches town. And once he's in Colts Run Cross we may never be able to find him."

Aidan spun the wheel and took off down the drive.

ZACH PARKED behind the old Colts Run Cross Elementary School where he had agreed to meet Tony. He walked cautiously to one of the back metal doors that had come unhinged at the top and had tilted to the side at a precarious angle. He squeezed though and stood just inside. His hand rested on the butt of his pistol as his eyes adjusted to the dingy dimness.

The building had stood empty since before Zach was born, but like most kids who'd grown up around here, he'd sneaked into the building on at least a couple of occasions. Usually it was to smoke swiped cigarettes when they were way too young to buy them, or to take turns sipping whiskey someone had sneaked from their parent's liquor cabinet.

Even when the old school wasn't the hangout for a killer, this wasn't the safest place to be. Most of the small, high windows had been shot out by teenage boys engaged in felonious target practice, and pieces of glass were scattered about the classroom floors. Bats thrived in the dark hallways and roaches, scorpions and spiders had taken up residence in the rusted desks left piled against rotting walls. Zach wondered if Tony had been holed up here ever since last Friday night when he'd put two bullets in Louisa Kellogg's head. It was fitting— one more rat in a building that crawled with them.

There was no sign of Tony as of yet, but he'd stay out of sight until he was certain Zach had come alone, as instructed. Zach waited five minutes before his impatience got the better of him. "If you're here, you better show your face," he called. "I didn't come out here to grow old." His voice echoed, the words bouncing off the walls like some cacophonous rap song.

Finally, Tony stepped from behind a rickety stairwell. He was unshaven and his clothes looked as if he'd slept in them for days.

He ambled toward Zach. "Did you bring the money?"

"I have it. We need to talk first."

"I told you everything. I'm being railroaded. I didn't kill those women."

"The forensics lab says your hairs were found on the black skirt Louisa Kellogg wore to work the night she was killed."

"They're lying. I'm being framed."

"Were you ever in the coffee shop where she worked?"

"Yeah, sure, I've been in there with Gerald. It's just around the corner from his house, but I wasn't there Friday night. I wasn't even in Houston."

"DNA tests don't lie."

"Cops do." Sweat broke out on Tony's forehead and his jowls swelled as though he was hoarding walnuts in them. "I'm counting on you, Zach. You started this when you went to my son's house and made him think

I'm some kind of murdering pervert. Now he won't help me. He won't have nothing to do with me."

Tony was crumbling like the old building, falling apart right in front of Zach. If it weren't for the DNA match, Zach might have worked up some sympathy for him.

"Why did you kill her, Tony? Were you high on something?"

"I swear I didn't kill anybody."

"You were mad at Gordon for not leaving you the ranch, weren't you? You were afraid if Kali or Hade got the ranch they'd find the bodies and you'd get caught. But if Hade went to jail for the murders and you killed Kali, you'd be home free."

"No. It wasn't like that. I should have inherited the ranch. I was the only one who stood by Gordon when he was dying. Just me. Nobody else. Not Hade. Not Kali. Just me. But I swear I didn't kill those women. You gotta believe me. You gotta help me or I'm dead meat."

"I'd like to believe you, but you haven't told me how your hairs got on Louisa's skirt."

"I told you, they were planted, probably by some crooked detective bucking to get his name in print. Someone like Aidan Jefferies. He's tried to be the big shot in all of this."

"Aidan wouldn't do that."

"Well, then it was someone else. Just give me the money I asked you for, Zach. You got more than the Queen of England and you owe it to me for turning my own flesh and blood against me. I got a man all lined up to fly me to Mexico City, but Gerald won't even take my calls."

"I don't owe you anything, Tony Pinter." Zach pulled his Glock and pointed it at a spot right between Tony's eyes. "I'm taking you in for the murder of Louisa Kellogg."

"You filthy, lowdown, swine of a liar. You're no cop."

"So I've been told."

Tony turned and started running up the staircase, his back to Zach as if daring him to shoot. Zach aimed, but his finger froze on the trigger. He couldn't shoot a man in the back.

He raced for the stairs, but by the time Tony had reached the landing, he'd pulled a gun of his own. The first bullet ricocheted off the step by Zach's foot, flying into the wall and creating a rain of shattered plaster.

Zach fired back and kept running. He should have known Tony would be armed, but it didn't matter. He'd have taken him on anyway. This had to end. The next woman who died might well be Kali.

KALI HAD CAUGHT several glimpses of Zach's car on the highway, but they lost him completely once he reached Colt Run's Cross. She'd tried his phone a half dozen times with no luck.

Aidan took out his phone. "I'll try Langston."

Kali could only hear Aidan's side of the conversation, but she could tell that he was getting nowhere.

"Apparently Zach didn't tell anyone he was leaving or where he was going," Aidan said. "He could be anywhere, and I don't know this town all that well."

"Neither do I, but we have to keep looking. The town's not that big. Just drive around and see if we spot his car."

They cruised the old downtown section. It was crowded with Saturday-afternoon shoppers and tourists who drove out from Houston on weekends to browse the antique shops.

"Turn down that street," she said, pointing right when they reached the corner.

Aidan swerved into the turn lane. "Did you see his car?"

"No, but I think that's where the town park is. He could be meeting Tony there."

"We don't even know for certain that he's meeting Tony."

She couldn't argue the point, but she was growing edgier by the second. She'd been right about the location of the park. It was filled with kids playing soccer and mothers pushing their youngsters in swings and watching their toddlers crawl through bright-red plastic tunnels.

"I'd have a better chance of finding him in Houston," Aidan said. "There are millions of people, but the criminals tend to haunt the same poverty-stricken areas."

"There has to be a wrong side of the tracks here, too," Kali said. "I just don't know where to look for it. Just think of where a man like Tony might hide out."

"If I knew that, he'd have been arrested days ago." Aidan swerved the car into a U-turn and picked up speed. "But when we were looking for him, Ed did take me to some areas more promising than this one."

Aidan turned north at a stop sign, then left at the next corner and went straight a half mile before turning on a blacktop road that appeared to lead nowhere.

"This is the oldest section of town," Aidan said. "There's an empty warehouse down this road and some abandoned houses. We checked them all out two days ago, but we could have missed something."

"I'll watch out the right side of the car, you watch out the left," Kali said, her gaze fixed on a stucco building just ahead. "Pull in here? He could have parked in the back of the building."

Aidan jumped the curve and sped over a cracked gravel parking lot until they had a view of the back of the building. There was nothing there but the body of a rusted-out Chevy that was older than Kali.

Her optimism nose-dived. Zach could be any-where, in danger or merely blowing off steam. Every law-enforcement officer in the county had been searching their own turf for Tony Pinter for days and they hadn't found him. What chance did she and Aidan have to find Zach?

Her frustration transformed to anger. "Why would Zach run off like this without saying where he was going? Why would he take on Tony by himself?"

"He's a Collingsworth, Kali. All four of the brothers are like that. It's in their blood. They never back down from what they believe is right. They never quit on a friend, either, or fail to protect the women they love."

But Kali didn't want Zach to wind up a dead Collingsworth hero. She wanted him alive.

"What's that building?" she asked as they approached a two-story structure with broken windows and surrounded by weeds and thigh-high grass.

"A rat trap now. It used to be a school. We checked it out the other day. It's dank and moldy and crawling with vermin. I doubt even Tony would brave that dump."

"Let's check it anyway."

This time he didn't have to jump the curb. There was a strip of cracked asphalt that ran to the back of the building. Kali lowered her window and stuck her head out for a better view.

Her heart slammed into her chest when she saw the silver Jag parked along the back edge of the drive.

Aidan dropped a couple of curse words. "Looks like you called it right, Kali. There's only one reason Zach would come to a place like this."

He put the car in Park and killed the engine. "Stay in the car and keep your head down unless I signal you differently."

"Why can't I go in with you?"

"Because I'm a cop and I said so." He pulled his gun, opened the door and stepped out of the car. Her heart was hammering against the walls of her chest as Aidan walked toward the back door of the school.

If Zach had somehow found out that Tony was here and come for a showdown with him, why was he still inside? Had Tony lured Zach out here to kill him? The questions bombarded her mind until she grew dizzy dealing with the fearful possibilities.

Aidan slipped inside the school and she held her breath willing him to find Zach unharmed. A bird sang in the tree above her. A dog barked in the distance. And gunfire cracked like exploding fireworks inside the school. Her insides rocked sickeningly, and she jumped from the car and ran toward the door Aidan had just walked through.

Aidan grabbed her when she entered and pushed her behind him.

"Up here, Aidan."

The air rushed from Kali's lungs at the sound of Zach's voice. She stepped from behind Aidan and quickly spotted him at the top of the warped metal staircase. His shirt was covered in blood.

"Where's Tony?" Aidan asked, his voice so strained she wouldn't have recognized it. But Kali didn't wait for an answer. She raced up the steps, fighting tears and fear and hatred for Tony Pinter.

Zach opened his arms and gathered her inside them. "It's okay. In fact, it's great."

"You're shot."

"No, this isn't my blood. I was just standing too close to the action."

Aidan joined them, his gun still in hand. "What happened here?"

"Nothing much. There wasn't a cop around so I apprehended your suspect for you. He's in there," Zach said, motioning to the open door of a classroom. "You may want to call an ambulance. He's lost a lot of blood. You can thank me later. Kali and I are going home."

THE MOOD was ecstatic and Kali felt as if this were her real homecoming to the Silver Spurs. The stars seemed brighter. The air seemed crisper. The evening sounds seemed friendlier. Best of all, Zach was his fun-loving, high-spirited self. It was the kind of night memories were made of.

The neighboring ranchers and wranglers had gone, but the Collingsworth clan was still on the scene, sitting around the folding tables in Kali's yard. The majority of the food had been cleared away. Only a few decadent desserts remained.

"I'd call this a successful day all around," Matt said. "Kali's new stable is up and finished except for a few final touches that we can take care of next weekend. And our psycho killer is behind bars."

"What a relief," Lenora said. "But I'm glad I didn't know you were going face-to-face with him, Zach."

"We're glad she didn't know, too," Jaime said. "She'd have marched us all over there to help and I just had my nails done." Jaime stepped behind Zach and wrapped her arms around his neck, her actions defying her words.

"He should have taken someone with him,"

Lenora said. "That's why I had four sons, so you'd be there for one another."

"Did you hear that, Trish?" Langston scooted his chair closer to his wife's and placed the palm of his hand on her shirt-covered belly. "Four sons is the perfect number."

"Can we just take this one at a time?"

But when Trish placed her hand over Langston's and looked up at him, Kali was sure she'd never seen such love in a woman's eyes. Unless it was in her own.

"I still can't believe Tony thought he could persuade you to give him money to skip the country," Matt said. "The guy had to be crazy even to chance calling you and telling you where he was."

"I think it was just desperation." Zach tipped his chair back, balancing it on two legs with his weight against one of the tables. "His tale of being framed for a crime he didn't commit was so convincing, I might have believed him if I hadn't known about the DNA match."

"I'm just glad it ended like it did," Langston said, "with you alive, though I can't say I'd be all that upset if you'd killed Tony."

"It probably would have come down to that if the bat hadn't swooped down from the ceiling at that exact moment."

"Swatting at a bat, tripping and falling on a shard of glass from a broken windowpane, and then having the glass spear clear his heart by mere inches. How ironic is that?" Bart asked.

"It's the way it was meant to be," Bart's wife said. "The wound will heal and he'll go to trial for murdering Louisa Kellogg and likely the other women, too. Even Zach's leading him to justice is poetic. He said he'd protect Kali, and he did."

Kali loved the way Jaclyn made everything sound as if it were part of a divine plan. Only, where did the plan go now for her and Zach? They'd moved from friends to lovers in the whirlwind of danger. But what happened now that he had no reason to spend his days at her side and his nights in her bed?

"I hate to break up a good party," Lenora said, "but I have to get back to Jack's Bluff and Jeremiah so that Juanita can get home to her family. She was a dear to offer to stay with him this late."

"I'm ready to call it a day, too," Bart said. "Swinging that hammer all day took it out of me."

The others stood, as well, saying their goodbyes to Kali and Zach as if it were assumed he'd stay with her again tonight. But she knew they must be wondering how long he'd stay on in her humble abode when he had the big house at Jack's Bluff to go home to.

Zach put his arm around Kali's waist as his family walked away. She leaned into him, determined not to ruin the most perfect night of her life worrying about tomorrow.

He pulled her into his arms as the last car pulled away. "What do you think of the stable? Were you surprised?"

"I was totally shocked and I love it. I just never expected anything so nice."

"Only costs twice as much to go first class," he teased. "Unless you're taking a commercial flight. Then it takes ten times as much."

And even then the Collingsworths could afford first class. "How much do I owe you?"

"Come take a shower with me. I'm sure I can think of some way you can repay me."

He was only teasing, but the connotation still stung. She made love with him because it was the most satisfying and thrilling thing she'd ever experienced, not because she wanted anything in return.

"I want to pay you for the materials, Zach."

"It's a gift."

"Candy or flowers are gifts. This is a permanent structure for my ranch."

"One you lost through no fault of your own. Besides, I can easily afford it and you said yourself, you need your money to buy horses."

He could afford the stable and a hundred more like it and probably never even glance at the invoice. That wasn't the point. She couldn't explain her feelings and trying made her sound ungrateful. "I honestly love the new stable and I appreciate your wanting to do it for me. I just feel better about things when I pay my own way."

He shrugged and let his arms fall back to his side. "Okay. I'll send you an invoice." He stretched and massaged the back of his neck. "I'm beat. I need a hot shower and a nice comfortable bed to crawl into."

And the closest comfortable bed was at Jack's Bluff. "With Tony in jail, there's no reason I can't stay by myself if you'd rather sleep in your own bed tonight. I know my mattress needs replacing."

"Do you want me to leave, Kali? Is that what this is about?"

"No, of course not. I was just thinking of you."

"I'm here because I like being with you. Otherwise I'd leave."

But he didn't touch her as they walked inside and as her perfect night began to shatter, she had a heartbreaking premonition that things between them would never be the same.

Chapter Fifteen

Zach spread the Sunday edition of the *Houston Chronicle* on the kitchen table and turned to the sports pages. He started reading an article about the Rockets' chances of making the NBA playoffs this year, but couldn't concentrate.

He was edgy from too much caffeine and bummed out with guilt. He'd left the Silver Spurs that morning without waking Kali to tell her he was leaving or to kiss her goodbye. He'd simply crawled from the bed after a restless night, wrote her a note that said he'd call later and headed back to Jack's Bluff.

It was a copout. He knew it and he wasn't proud of it. But things had gotten sticky last night and he'd never been good at handling complications in a romantic liaison. He'd thought Kali would be thrilled about having her stable replaced. Instead she'd shunned the gift, acting as if he'd been trying to buy her.

He didn't see why doing things for someone you cared about was a crime. But if she wanted an invoice, he'd give her one. Like the money made any difference to him.

The problem was that their relationship had heated up too fast. The passion had been heightened by the danger, and the two had fused to create a combustible dynamic that was bound to either explode or cool down.

They'd reached that point last night when the danger had suddenly been put to rest. It was as if she wanted some kind of commitment from him with all her talk of his no longer having to be there. He wasn't ready for that. He might never be.

But he did like it when they were together. Making love with her had been one of the top thrills of his life. And he'd had more than his share of electrifying moments, from skydiving to safaris in the African bush.

Langston stuck his head through the kitchen door. "Have you seen Gina?"

"Not since brunch."

"Well, if you see her, tell her I'm looking for her."

"Is anything wrong?"

"No, but I promised to go horseback riding with her when I finished returning some phone calls and I'm ready to go."

"If I see her, I'll pass the word along."

Langston walked over to the table and wrapped his hands around the top rung of the chair opposite Zach. "I talked to Aidan a few minutes ago."

"Did he say anything about Tony Pinter?"

"Only that he's going to survive his wound and he's still proclaiming his innocence long and loud. He's admitted that he and his son were in the coffee shop where Louisa Kellogg worked a few nights before she was killed, but insists that he was home alone that Friday night."

"Gerald Pinter said he hadn't seen his father in weeks."

"One of them has to be lying," Langston said. "I'd put my money on Tony for that."

"I'd say you're probably right."

"Aidan did ask me to give you a message, though. He said that he still stands by his statement that you'd make a hell of a cop and to tell you that the HPD is hiring."

Zach nodded and went back to the article on the Rockets.

Gina came bounding into the kitchen in her stocking feet with Blackie dancing at her heels. "Can we go riding now?"

"Yeah," Langston said. "Get your boots on. I'll be right there." He waited until she was gone then turned back to Zach.

"You're not actually thinking of going to work for the HPD, are you?"

"Haven't given it a thought."

"Good. Collingsworth Oil needs you and you can write your own ticket there without being shot at by drug dealers and psychos."

Langston left, but Zach gave up on the newspa-

per. The relationship between Tony and his son
Gerald was a strange one. It didn't make sense that
Gerald would turn on his father just because Aidan
and Zach had stopped by his house asking about
Tony's whereabouts. Tony was likely lying about
that. But then it was odd for Tony to pick up a woman
around the corner from his son's house when his son
claimed he hadn't seen his father in weeks.

Zach sat his coffee cup in the sink and went to get
his jacket.

"Are you going to Kali's?" his mother asked as he
started out the door.

"No, I'm driving into Houston."

"Any special reason?"

"I need a cup of coffee."

THE COFFEE SHOP where Louisa Kellogg had worked
before her murder was bustling when Zach arrived.
All the outside tables were full in spite of the fact that
Houston skies had turned gray and overcast. Unlike
most of the coffee houses he'd been in lately, this one
actually had waitresses. He took a table all the way
at the back.

"Can I help you?"

"I hope so."

The young blond waitress smiled flirtatiously.
"All depends on what you want."

"A small black coffee and some information. I tip
big."

"Oh! Not another one." She stuffed her hands in

her pockets and shuffled her feet. "Are you a cop or a reporter?"

"Is one better than the other?"

"You're a cop. You have that look. Ask away, but make it fast. My boss likes us to keep moving."

"Have you ever seen the man who was arrested for Louisa Kellogg's murder in here before?"

"Occasionally, but his son's a regular. He lives nearby, I think. His name's Gerald. He's told me that a bunch of times."

"What's he like?"

"Tony Pinter?"

"No, his son."

"He's okay, not much of a tipper. He asks a lot of questions when he's being waited on."

"What kind of questions?"

"What kind of music do I like? What do I read? Do I live with my parents? I think he's just trying to be friendly, but some of the waitresses don't like him because they say he looks at them funny. I'd rather have funny looks than those guys who try to look down your shirt when you put their coffee on the table. Old men are the worst about that."

"Did you work the Friday night Louisa was murdered?"

"Yeah. I keep thinking it could have been me. Luckily I had to work until eleven."

"Was Tony Pinter in the Friday night Louisa was killed?"

She glanced around nervously, probably to see if

her boss was watching. "Detective Jefferies already asked us all that."

Zach slapped a couple of twenties on the table. "And your answer was?"

"No. He'd come in a few nights before with Gerald. I know because I waited on them. That's the night Gerald went schizo."

"What brought that on?"

"Evidently he'd loaned his father a pullover sweater because when his father sloshed a few drops of coffee on the sleeve, Gerald started talking to him like he was stupid. I guess Gerald must be a neatness freak or something."

"And this was a few nights before Louisa was murdered?"

"Yeah, the Tuesday before, I think. Anyway I carry one of those eraser cleansers." She pulled it out of her pocket to show Zach. "I got the stain right out. He probably didn't even have to wash it before he wore it again.

"Oh, yeah and one more thing. Gerald's always got this bottle of little white pills in his pocket. I don't know what they are, but when he takes them, his eyes kind of glaze over. That might be why the other waitresses think he looks at them funny." She looked around again. "I'm getting the look. I've gotta get moving. Did you say a small black coffee?"

"Skip the coffee. I've already got what I came for." He slipped the two twenties back in his wallet and removed a hundred-dollar bill. "Have a nice day," he said pressing the bill into her hand. "And stay away from Gerald Pinter."

I'LL call you.

It was the quintessential breakup note. Kali would have expected something a bit more creative from Zach Collingsworth. But he'd been in such a hurry to clear out he hadn't even made coffee.

It was her own fault. She'd warned herself over and over not to lose her heart to him.

Only, how could she help it?

He was not only breathtakingly handsome, he was also charming and funny and so much more. He'd been her protector and her lover. But when it was all said and done, the best he could offer was the fact that he liked being with her.

But he wasn't with her now and he hadn't called. She checked her cell phone for at least the hundredth time that day. It was working fine. She was the one who was falling apart.

She had the ranch and with it the chance to make her dream of breeding and training horses come true. Hade Carpenter was out of her life. And the killer who'd made a nightmare of her life was behind bars. She should be walking on air, not fighting tears over a love affair that had never really had a chance. She and Zach might both get their mail at a Colts Run Cross address but they lived in two different worlds.

She hugged the phone to her chest and then tossed it to the sofa. Enough was enough. She was going for a walk and if Zach happened to call, she wouldn't be available to answer.

"Come on, Chideaux. Let's go exploring our new ranch."

The puppy played at her heels until they neared the new stable, then he started barking and growling as if he thought the new structure was some kind of evil apparition.

"It's part of the ranch, now, Chideaux. That's where our horses will stay when they're not out in the pastures or being ridden."

Chideaux barked all the more frantically, digging his front feet into the ground and looking as though he was ready to attack. Finally, she had to pick him up and carry him past the stable so she could get on with the walk.

Not that the walk was helping. She missed Zach more with every step.

ADRENALINE was pumping through him at the speed of light by the time Zach reached his car. He gunned the engine and pulled into the street, then punched in Kali's cell phone number. There was no answer.

He called again. Still no answer. Apprehension hit like an electric current, going through every nerve in his body at once. He called again and this time he left her a message to call him back immediately. There was a new development in the murder case that could change everything.

The wrong Pinter might be in jail.

It was Tony's hairs, but that didn't mean he was wearing the sweater when Louisa Kellogg was murdered.

Zach tried Kali's number again. This time when she didn't answer, he called Ed Guerra's direct line. Everything was probably fine, but he wanted a deputy at Kali's house immediately. As Aidan said, you never know what a psycho will do.

KALI AND Chideaux were gone for well over an hour, though she didn't walk the entire time. She'd happened onto a pond she'd either forgotten since sixth grade or never knew about. It was the perfect spot for trail-ride picnics and she'd sat in the sun next to the water and tried to lose herself in plans for the future.

It had helped for a while, but now the stable loomed in front of her and thoughts of Zach came crashing down on her like falling rocks. She could lie to herself all she wanted about being fine without him. She wouldn't be. She loved him, and she'd miss him for a long, long time.

Now that she'd admitted it, she felt even worse.

Chideaux ran up to the stable and started his frantic barking and growling again. Only this time he squeezed through a narrow crack where the door hadn't closed completely and disappeared inside. She was almost sure that door had been fully shut before.

A portentous foreboding brought gooseflesh to her arms and made the hair rise on the back of her neck. She scanned the area and then breathed easier when she spotted a county sheriff's squad car parked at the side of her drive. One of the deputies must have stopped by to see the new stable. Word traveled fast in Colts Run Cross. She'd have to get used to that.

She walked over and swung open the door to see which lawman had come calling. She stared into the dimness. There was no one there. Something sharp pieced her side and she felt a rivulet of hot blood run down her skin. And then she saw the man.

"Hello, Kali. Looks like I finally get you all to myself."

She screamed.

The knife pierced deeper. "If you're yelling for the nice young deputy, you needn't bother. A dead man is no help at all."

Chapter Sixteen

The man grabbed Kali around the neck, confining her in a stranglehold while he sliced her denim skirt from the waist to the hem. Kali shuddered as the skirt pooled at her feet and jagged pieces of the horrifying puzzle began to fall into place.

"You're the one who killed those women, aren't you?"

"Smart lady. Too bad the cops weren't as smart. They would have known my father would never kill a woman. He only married them and let them treat him like scum."

"You're Tony Pinter's son?"

"Does that surprise you?"

His grip tightened until her lungs burned and she felt as if her head were wobbling. Chideaux had tried to warn her. She'd ignored his barking, blinded by the certainty that the killer was behind bars.

But he wasn't barking now. She tried to move her head, but his hold on her was too tight. "Where's my puppy?"

"You'd best worry about yourself."

She jerked her leg trying to kick backward and knock him off balance. His hand jerked, but the movement only made the knife slice into her flesh.

"Swallow these," Gerald said, stuffing a handful of tiny white pills into her mouth. "They'll make you better company for me."

She tried to spit them out, but he held her mouth closed and tilted her head until she was sure a few of them had worked their way down her throat.

"Can you imagine what it feels like to be sliced like a piece of meat, Kali? Have you ever wondered what it's like when the cuts are so deep and so numerous that your flesh looks like red fabric?"

Oh, God. He was truly crazy or else he was high on some kind of mind-altering drug. Either way, this was a game to him, a cold, cruel game. She had to stay focused. Had to read him the way she read horses when they lashed out in fear and frustration. Her only chance to live was to best him at the mind games.

The knife exited the wound and then slid down her side only to prick her in a new spot. Tears filled her eyes and she bit hard into her bottom lip to help her stand the pain. The blood was soaking her panties. She had to think fast or she'd be dead.

She finally spotted Chideaux. He was lying motionless on the floor at the edge of one of the stalls. Her stomach rolled.

"You wanted the ranch, Kali. Now it's yours. You

can live on it forever. Well, not live actually, but you will be part of the land."

A siren sounded in the distance. His face twisted as if he were fighting a blinding migraine. Finally he dropped his hand from around her neck though the blade of the knife was still jabbing into her.

If she was going to make a move, she'd have to make it now while he was distracted and before she lost too much blood. She took a painful breath and drew on all her strength. With one quick movement, she lunged for the door.

The knife fell away, but Gerald grabbed fistfuls of her hair and slammed her against the heavy wood. A shower of needles exploded in her brain. He pushed her against the wall, but this time he slid the blade of the knife to a spot just above her collar bone.

"You shouldn't have stolen the ranch from my father, Kali. You should have stayed away. Then I wouldn't have had to kill you."

"You don't have to kill me. You never had to kill anyone."

His face turned red. "You're wrong. You see, the stress builds up in my head and it just keeps building until I find release. Most people don't know it, but murder is a great stress reliever."

He was totally insane and he was going to kill her right here in her new wonderful stable. She should have never come to the Silver Spurs. No one could save her now. Not even Zach.

The one thing she didn't regret about coming to

the Silver Spurs was falling in love with him even though she'd never get the chance to tell him that.

ZACH HEARD the siren coming from somewhere behind him as he pulled though the gate at the Silver Spurs. It made him nervous simply because he still hadn't been able to reach Kali. But Guerra had assured him when he'd called that Chester Maxwell was already in the area and he'd have the deputy stop in to make sure Kali was fine. If anything had been wrong, Zach would surely have heard by now.

His initial panic in not being able to reach her had made him do some soul-searching. He shouldn't have needed another episode of danger to realize how he felt about Kali, but he was hard-headed, and his fear of commitment had been with him a long time. Old habits were hard to break.

They'd start over, go slower so that he could court her the way she deserved.

The siren grew louder. It had to be close behind him. A new wave of anxiety rode his nerves. He pressed his foot against the accelerator pedal, pushing his speed as fast as he could without going airborne on the bumpy road.

He breathed a little easier when he saw a sheriff's squad car parked in front of Kali's house, but still he grabbed his pistol and jumped from the car the second the car stopped. He rushed up the walk and was about to open the door when he saw the stream of blood spilling over the threshold and onto the porch.

His heart crashed against his chest with hammer-like force. Not Kali. Please don't let the blood be Kali's. His hands were shaking as he pushed open the door and shoved it into the dead weight of Deputy Chester Maxwell.

"Kali!"

He yelled her name as he made a quick search of the house and then ran out the back door. Every nerve in his body was screaming for him to do something, but he had no idea where to search first.

He called her name again, his voice almost swallowed up in the siren that was right on top of him, probably pulling into Kali's drive.

The siren shut off and he heard the sorrowful wail of a dog coming from the direction of the stable. Chideaux. Zach took off running, afraid even to think of what he might find.

THE SIREN had stopped. Another deputy must have arrived. Gerald would have to kill him, too, the way he should have killed the howling mutt. Instead he'd wasted his precious pills on him. He'd always hated the thought of hurting a dog.

He let go of Kali and took his place just behind the door, the knife ready to plunge into the deputy's chest.

KALI WAS FADING in and out of consciousness. The pills. Or the loss of blood. She had to focus.

"Kali!"

It was Zach. He was coming to save her. Or else

she was dreaming. She tried to swallow. Her mouth was too dry. Gerald was standing by the door holding the knife over his head. Ready to kill…

Ready to kill Zach. Panic swirled through her muddled mind flashing on and off like neon signs. She had to warn Zach.

"He's waiting with a knife." The scream felt like broken glass when it flew from her dry throat. Gerald lunged for her with the extended blade. She crumpled and fell as the sound of a bullet put out the neon lights and cleared her mind.

ZACH RUSHED to Kali, jumping over Gerald's body to reach her. He knelt beside her and cradled her in his arms, his heart all but stopping when his hand touched her bloody shirt. He checked her side. There were three wounds, all of them oozing but no severe bleeding. Her eyes were glazed and the pupils dilated. "Hang on, baby. I'm here and it's all right. I'll take care of you."

Ed Guerra burst through the door. "What's going on? What happened to Kali? And who is that?" he said motioning to Gerald's body.

"That's your serial killer. The bastard also killed Chester Maxwell. Kali's been drugged and lost some blood. I'll answer the rest of your questions later. Right now I'm getting the woman I love to a doctor."

He gathered her in his arms and carried her outside. "I should have been here, Kali. I should have been with you."

She could have told him that fifteen years ago.

Epilogue

Three weeks later

Lenora slipped from the house just after daybreak with a bouquet of daffodils in her arms. Randolph hadn't been much of a flower man, but he'd liked daffodils. She took the worn path to the oldest oak tree and settled in the grass near his grave.

"It's a gorgeous spring morning, Randolph. You'd have a lot to celebrate if you were here, but Zach would no doubt be stealing your thunder. He's Colts Run Cross's favorite hero since he single-handedly took out a serial killer who'd been burying his victims on the Silver Spurs Ranch for the past four years.

"Can you imagine how it makes me feel to know a man like that has been little more than a stone's throw from Jaime and Becky all this time? I guess we'll never know what drove Gerald Pinter over the edge, since he's dead, but then I'm not sure we ever know what causes any person to take someone else's life.

"But Kali Cooper is a sweet girl, down to earth and gutsy and she's crazy about Zach. The feeling is mutual. She doesn't have to worry about Hade Carpenter anymore, either. He's confessed to arson and stealing tractors and implements from the ranch. His sentence will be reduced since he plea-bargained, but I don't think we'll see him anywhere around Colts Run Cross when he gets out of prison.

"I'm not sure what's going to come of that business with the CIA, but I know that Langston will get to the bottom of it. Oh, and one more bit of news. Langston and Trish are going to have a son. Langston says they'll name him after you. That's a good omen. I'd like to think that long after we're gone, our influence will live on in our kids and grandkids right on down through time. Speaking of kids, I do hope Matt finds a woman he can love and start a family with soon. He has so much to give. See if you can help out with that, will you?

"And Happy Sixtieth birthday, my love. You should have had so many, many more."

KALI STOOD at the door watching for Zach. He had been so secretive about tonight that her curiosity was driving her to delirium. He'd said she should expect company that would excite and stimulate her even though she'd never let him in her house.

She'd never met a male who excited and stimulated her more than Zach, but she loved having him in her house. She was still in awe that they could be from such different backgrounds and yet get along so well. Not that they didn't still have their differences. He was hard-headed. She had a quick temper. He liked life on the edge. She liked things organized with fewer surprises—except in bed. They were equally experimental and passionate there. He had moved back to Jack's Bluff after she'd recovered from her incident with Gerald Pinter, but they'd spent almost every weekend together.

He'd never mentioned marriage, but then she'd never expected him to. Loving didn't change the fact that they were worlds apart.

Money was still their most troublesome issue. He didn't understand why she wouldn't just let him write a check for everything she wanted or needed for the ranch. She'd stood by her guns. If the ranch had belonged to both of them it would have been different. The way things stood now, he would essentially be giving handouts to her.

She'd just stepped away from the window when Chideaux started barking. He was much better than a doorbell for letting her know when someone was around. She opened the door and rushed to the porch, then sucked in a quick breath. Zach had just arrived in a black pickup truck pulling a horse trailer.

Surely he hadn't bought her a horse after all their talks about money. But she watched as he went to the back of the trailer and unloaded a magnificent, high-stepping, spirited palomino. He knew full well how difficult it would be to say no to this.

"So what do you think?" he asked, when she joined them at the end of the walk. "Does he excite and stimulate you like I promised?"

"You know that he does." She ran her down the horse's aristocratic neck.

"He's a purebred," Zach said. "He'll be perfect for breeding and showing."

"Oh, Zach, you have got to stop this. He's so beautiful. I love him already, but you know I can't afford him."

"Nobody said he was yours. He's mine."

She shook her head. "Only, you want to leave him in my stable?"

"I didn't say that. Now, I have a question for you. How do you feel about sleeping with a detective?"

"Detective, as in cop?"

"As in deputy detective with the County Sheriffs Department. I'd have to go through the training program, but Ed Guerra says I have just the kind of investigative mind he's looking for to head a new Special Crimes Unit. What do you think?"

"I'm flabbergasted. What about the position at Collingsworth Oil?"

"I've talked to Langston and explained that the oil business just doesn't cut it for me. I like what Aidan does. He collects evidence, examines the clues and solves the puzzle. Then he makes the arrest and takes the criminal off the street. I like the logic of that. It feels right for me. And don't worry about the cut in pay. I'll still own one-eighth of Collingsworth Enterprises, so I can afford to treat you to a steak every now and then—or a trip to Venice for our honeymoon."

"Venice? For our honeymoon." She was surely missing something here.

"Unless you'd rather go to Paris or Luckenbach, Texas. Any place you want is fine by me." He took her hand and bent down on one knee.

Her head was spinning. This couldn't be real.

"I love you, Kali Cooper. I love your laugh, your wild hair, the freckles on your nose, the way you kiss and make love. I love everything about you. I thought I was afraid of commitment, but the truth was, I was waiting for you."

"Oh, Zach. I love you so much, so very, very much."

"Then marry me, Kali. Marry me so we can fill the Silver Spurs Ranch with horses, kids and love—and so that I can keep my new palomino in your stable."

"You mean *our* new palomino in *our* stable."

"Exactly."

"Yes! Yes, I'll marry you, Zach Collingsworth. I can't wait to be your wife."

Tears filled her eyes as he slipped a ring on her finger and took her in his arms. She'd come to Colt Runs Cross hoping to find a stable full of dreams. Instead she'd learned that dreams live only in the heart.

* * * * *

Turn the page for a first look at
the next book in the
FOUR BROTHERS OF COLTS RUN CROSS
series, Loaded.
Coming August 2009 only from
Mills & Boon® Intrigue.

Loaded

by

Joanna Wayne

Shelly Lane walked into the Kuntry Kookin' Kafé at
one-forty on Thursday afternoon in the middle of
June, following close on the heels of Matt Collingsworth. Smells of fried chicken, cinnamon and freshly
brewed coffee greeted her. It looked like the sort of
place you should seat yourself, but a short, plump
woman with a knot of graying curls on top of her
head was smiling and sashaying toward her.

"Hi, there," the lady said, her charming Texas
drawl pulling her words into extra syllables. "You
can just sit anywhere, and Jill will be around to take
your order in a jiffy."

"Thanks." Shelly glanced around and noted that
she was the only one eating alone. Most of the cus-
tomers were family groups, though there were a few
tables with just cowboy types. Several looked her
way. Most grinned and nodded. A few waved. Colts
Run Cross was a very friendly town.

Shelly located Matt. He'd joined a group of men

and one supercute young lady at a table near a window. She chose a spot where she could observe him without making it too obvious, though she didn't mind his seeing her now that she was about to make contact with his mother.

The chair wobbled a bit as she slid it closer to the square wooden table covered in a blue plaid cloth. A simple vase holding two silk daisies sat in the middle, flanked by inexpensive salt and pepper shakers and a bottle of ketchup.

Her attention returned to Matt. He was far more handsome up close and personal than the likenesses she'd studied of him. His hair was short, dark brown and only slightly rumpled by the Western hat he'd been wearing before entering the restaurant. His jeans were worn but clean, and though she couldn't tell it now, she knew from stealthily following him about town that they showed off his lean, hard frame to perfection.

He glanced her way and smiled. A treacherous skip of her heart forced her to take a deep breath and regroup. Even the slightest attraction on her part could compromise her mission.

Jill stopped at Shelly's elbow. "The special today is fried chicken, mashed potatoes, gravy and pinto beans. That comes with corn bread or biscuits and a dish of peach cobbler and ice cream for dessert. Or you can order off the lunch menu. It's on the back."

Jill turned the menu over and tapped the offerings with her index finger. "What can I get you to drink?"

"Just water, please, with lemon."

"Sure thing."

Jill stopped off at Matt's table, flirting shamelessly with him and his cohorts. Not that Shelly blamed her. They all had that sexy cowboy mystique about them. It was even more potent than Shelly had expected, but she knew Matt Collingsworth was no simple cowboy. Nor was he your everyday Texas rancher.

Not only did his family own the second largest spread in Texas, but they were sole owners of Collingsworth Enterprises, which encompassed the operations of Jack's Bluff Ranch as well as Collingsworth Oil and its related subsidiaries. They had ties to some of the highest-ranking businessmen and politicians in this country and in other key oil-producing areas of the world.

The waitress arrived with the water and Shelly ordered a grilled chicken salad. She lingered over her food, finally leaving although Matt was still engaged in a very animated conversation with the others at his table.

The sun was blinding when she stepped out the door of the small café. She fished in her handbag for her sunglasses and put them on as she crossed the street to her dark blue nondescript sedan. She was opening the door when she spotted a black car rounding the corner and speeding toward her.

Sunlight glinted off the barrel of a revolver as it slid through the open window. Her instincts and training kicked in at the speed of light. She searched the empty streets for someone to warn, then hurriedly dived into the car. In a split second she'd yanked the car door shut and rolled onto the floor. Mere heartbeats later, the sound of gunfire, broken glass and bullets pinging against metal shattered the quiet afternoon.

The car had roared past and she could hear the footsteps and voices of people rushing from the nearby shops before she realized she'd been hit.

It felt as if a dozen wasps had all found the same spot on the back of her upper arm. Blood soaked the sleeve of her blouse. She stared, the unbelievable nature of the situation making the facts difficult to register. This couldn't have happened. She was CIA and so far undercover that not even her own mother knew she was in Texas.

Her car door swung open. "She's been shot," a female yelled.

But when Shelly looked up, she was staring straight into the dark, piercing eyes of Matt Collingsworth. Trouble had never been more ominous—or looked so good.

Passion. Power. Suspense.
It's time to fall under the spell
of Nora Roberts.

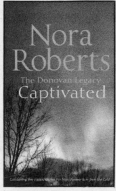

2nd January 2009

6th February 2009

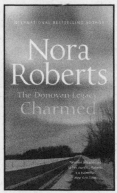

6th March 2009

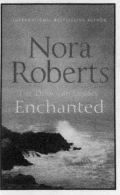

3rd April 2009

The Donovan Legacy
Four cousins. Four stories. One terrifying secret.

MILLS & BOON
INTRIGUE
On sale 19th June 2009

THE NEW DEPUTY IN TOWN
by BJ Daniels

Newly appointed Sheriff Nick Rogers is hiding out in Montana from his murderous ex-partner. Despite adopting the local lifestyle, he's completely out of his depth, especially when falling for Laney Cavanaugh might blow his cover.

OUT OF UNIFORM
by Catherine Mann

When Sergeant Jacob Stone opens his door to a mysterious woman without a past, he knows his time off is over. As threats to Dee's life bring her and Jacob together, she must learn to accept the help of a military hero with secrets of his own.

AROUND-THE-CLOCK PROTECTOR
by Jan Hambright

Rescuing Ava Ross should have been just like any other hostage mission. But when Carson Nash discovers Ava's four months pregnant – *with his child* – failure isn't an option!

LAST WOLF WATCHING
by Rhyannon Byrd

Brody Carter never acted on impulse – until he had to protect Michaela Doucet. A fiery psychic, she made him crazy and drew his hunger. Now, as they join forces to hunt down a threat to their pack, can Brody finally give in to his heart?

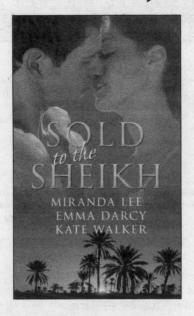

FREE!

2 Books
and a surprise gift!

We would like to take this opportunity to thank you for reading this Mills & Boon® book by offering you the chance to take TWO more specially selected titles from the Intrigue series absolutely FREE! We're also making this offer to introduce you to the benefits of the Mills & Boon® Book Club™—

- ★ **FREE home delivery**
- ★ **FREE gifts and competitions**
- ★ **FREE monthly Newsletter**
- ★ **Exclusive Mills & Boon Book Club offers**
- ★ **Books available before they're in the shops**

Accepting these FREE books and gift places you under no obligation to buy, you may cancel at any time, even after receiving your free shipment. Simply complete your details below and return the entire page to the address below. You don't even need a stamp!

YES! Please send me 2 free Intrigue books and a surprise gift. I understand that unless you hear from me, I will receive 4 superb new titles every month for just £3.19 each, postage and packing free. I am under no obligation to purchase any books and may cancel my subscription at any time. The free books and gift will be mine to keep in any case.

19ZEF

Ms/Mrs/Miss/Mr ....Initials...
BLOCK CAPITALS PLEASE

Surname...

Address...

....

....Postcode.......................................

Send this whole page to:
UK: FREEPOST CN81, Croydon, CR9 3WZ